Fiddle Fever

by *Sharon Arms Doucet*

Clarion Books
New York

Clarion Books
a Houghton Mifflin Company imprint
215 Park Avenue South, New York, NY 10003
Copyright © 2000 by Sharon Arms Doucet

The text was set in 13-point Adobe Garamond.

www.hmco.com/trade

Printed in USA.

Library of Congress Cataloging-in-Publication Data
Doucet, Sharon Arms.
Fiddle fever / by Sharon Arms Doucet.
p. cm.
Summary: In 1914, fourteen-year-old Félix LeBlanc feels stifled by life on his
family's farm in Louisiana, and after hearing his wayward uncle play the fiddle,
Félix decides that he wants to be a fiddler too, even if it means making his own
fiddle and going against his parents' wishes.
ISBN 0-618-04324-1
[1. Violin–Fiction. 2. Cajuns–Fiction. 3. Family life–Louisiana–Fiction.
4. Louisiana–Fiction.] I. Title.

PZ7. D7415 Fi 2000
[Fic]–dc21   00-025913

HAD 10 9 8 7 6 5 4 3 2 1

Dedicated to the memory of Creole fiddler
Canray Fontenot,
who made his first fiddle from a cigar box,
and to
Michael,
my fiddle man

Acknowledgments

Mille mercis to my editor, Michele Coppola, whose enthusiasm carried me through, and to my agent, Frances Kuffel, who believed from the beginning. Also to all my family, friends, and writing buddies who aided and abetted me in writing this book, including Carl Brasseux, Freddie Brooking, Barbara Conner, Ezra Doucet, Michael Doucet, Paul Fleischman, Will Hobbs, Ellen Howard, Colleen McDaniel, Jan Rider Newman, Peggy Nolan, Marc and Ann Savoy, the Silvey boys, Jane Vidrine, and Linda Arms White.

Contents

A Note from the Author

The late Creole fiddler Canray Fontenot, to whom this book is dedicated, once told me how he started playing music. The son of a popular accordion player, Canray wasn't interested in learning to play an instrument until, at the age of nine, he heard an old fiddler play one particular song that went straight to his heart. That day, Canray said, "Lord, that's what I want to do."

Canray's family had no money to buy him a fiddle, so he set about making one from a wooden cigar box. He used sewing thread instead of horsehair on the bow and screen wire for the strings. He learned to play his fiddle so well that his uncle finally gave him a real fiddle. Canray went on to play his French Creole music all over North America and Europe, winning numerous awards and even performing at concerts in New York's prestigious Carnegie Hall.

Canray's ingenuity and determination inspired me to write about Félix (pronounced *fay-LEEX*), the character in this book.

Félix and his family and friends all speak French because they are descendants of the French settlers who made their homes in *Acadie,* now the part of Canada known as Nova Scotia and New Brunswick. The Acadians, as they came to be called, lived there in peace and prosperity from 1604 until 1755. By then the French had ceded Acadia to the British, who tried to force the Acadians to swear allegiance to England. When they refused, their homes were burned, their lands were seized, and the people were loaded onto ships for deportation. Families were separated, and as many as one quarter of them died of hunger, disease, or shipwreck on their way to England, the American colonies, or the Caribbean.

After countless hardships, many of the remaining Acadians began arriving in Louisiana in the 1760s. The then-Spanish government gave them land grants along the bayous and prairies of southern Louisiana, and there the Acadians created new communities. The word *Acadian* was eventually shortened to *Cajun,* which is commonly used today. To this day, the Cajuns have stubbornly maintained their Catholic religion, their French language, and their love of family and music.

French music has kept its place as the heart and soul of the Cajun culture. It's been said that every Cajun is either a musician or a frustrated one, and dance floors in south Louisiana are important social centers. The music, loved by young and old alike, expresses the history of hardship, and the hope of the Cajun people. Today many young people are forming Cajun and zydeco bands, still finding modern voices in the time-honored words and melodies of their ancestors.

"Jacky, come and give me thy fiddle,
If ever thou mean to thrive."
"Nay, I'll not give my fiddle
To any man alive.

"If I should give my fiddle,
They'll think that I've gone mad;
For many a joyous day
My fiddle and I have had."

—from *The Real Mother Goose*

'Nonc Adolphe

When you get right down to it, a fiddle's nothing but a fancy wooden box wired up with strings. All by itself it can't do a darned thing but sit there in hollow silence. Then somebody comes along and draws a bow across those waiting strings and they start to quiver. The wood of the box takes in the strings' vibration and adds its own.

And in the right hands, out comes music.

It's by making music that the fiddle lets itself out, a self that lives in all that restless air inside it, and in the grain of the wood, and in the guts of its strings.

At the end of 1914, my life out on our Louisiana farm was as quiet as an empty box, and as flat as the vast prairie that stretched out to sundown beyond my bedroom window. But, like silent music in a neglected fiddle, I knew there was something sleeping inside of me, something at the heart of who I, Félix Octave LeBlanc, really was.

On a warm December night, two weeks before Christmas, my life broke out of its sleepy rut. And nothing was ever the same after that.

It was the night of the big house dance at my best friend Chance Guidry's. Chance and I had been talking about nothing else for days. For the first time Chance's daddy, Monsieur Guidry, had said we were old enough to stay up with the grownups instead of going to bed early with the little kids. And Papa had agreed.

I couldn't wait.

It was a three-mile wagon trek from our farm to Chance's. The night air was warm and muggy, meaning we'd soon get blasted by a winter storm from the north. We jostled down the road, our faces lit by the last of the pale winter sun.

Up on the wagon seat Papa smiled as if he'd just told himself a funny joke. Beside him sat Maman, her mouth set in a straight line, as usual, as if she'd just tasted something she didn't like. My little brother, Paulo, who was seven, hung over the side, catching at swirls of dust coming off the wheels. Every once in a while he'd get off a shot from the elderberry peashooter I'd made him, stinging my shoulder. "Too bad you'll have to go to bed with all the other babies tonight," I said in retaliation. "You'll miss all the fun." He stuck out his tongue, and I knew I had him.

But my pleasure in my triumph was forgotten the moment I spied lights up ahead. There, lit up like a Mississippi steamboat on the dark Louisiana prairie, sat the Guidrys' big white house. As we pulled into their yard, I saw Chance waving frantically from the gallery. My head buzzing with excitement, I hopped over the side of the wagon.

"Just a minute, Félix," said Maman from the buckboard. "Let me look at you."

"Aw, Maman," I said, but she proceeded to smooth my hair and rub my cheek with her thumb. She never stopped fussing over me, and since I'd turned fourteen, it had begun to drive me crazy.

Just then Chance lumbered up, looking like he was going to trip over his man-size feet. His dark eyes glinted with excitement. "You ain't never gonna guess who's here!" he said.

"Who—the governor?" I joked. He shook his head.

"The pope?" asked Papa.

"No, sir. Better than that." He stared at me a minute to let the suspense build. Finally, he pronounced, "It's your uncle!"

Behind me Maman gasped. "You mean Adolphe?" she said.

"The one and only," crowed Chance. "The best fiddler in the whole darn state of Louisiana. My daddy said he rode up bold as you please, still full of road dust, acting like he'd never even gone off and left. He's got his fiddle with him, too, and he's fixing to start playing any minute!"

As my mind tried to wrap itself around this news, I

looked up at Maman. The color had drained out of her cheeks, and she heaved a deep sigh as Papa put his arm around her. "Well, Marie," he said, "we better go see what that rascal's up to. Give me your hand."

Maman let him help her down, then reached for the black iron pot of her famous sausage *jambalaya* she'd brought for the supper. Her jaw was clenched so tight I saw the muscle jump under her cheek.

"Who are y'all talking about?" said Paulo, tumbling out of the wagon.

"Don't you know nothing?" I said. "It's 'Nonc Adolphe, back from wherever he went."

'Nonc Adolphe was Maman's brother. He had run off four years back, when I was only ten. It was the year of Halley's comet, when lots of people went a little crazy. Folks said 'Nonc Adolphe had gotten the comet fever. We hadn't heard from him since except for an occasional post-card from New Orleans or Houston, once even from St. Louis. And he'd left my parents in a pretty big fix.

When my grandfather died, Maman and 'Nonc Adolphe had split up the Olivier family farm, where they and two generations of Oliviers before them had been born. 'Nonc got the big old house and the high land around it, with good stands of oak and pecan trees and a clear, cool spring. Maman got the low land along the bayou, which washed away in the spring floods and bred world-class mosquitoes year-round.

On the LeBlanc side, Papa was the youngest of seven LeBlanc brothers and had gotten last choice of plots when their farm was divided up. So the farm where he'd built our house was a rough parcel of hardpan clay. Papa spent his life struggling to make a living off of two raw deals.

So when 'Nonc Adolphe disappeared without a word four years back, leaving all that good land to grow up in weeds and the old house neglected, Maman and Papa didn't look too kindly on it. Papa wouldn't dream of farming another man's land without his permission, plus we never knew when 'Nonc might come back. So we just kept working away, with 'Nonc's high acreage grinning at us like a carrot on a stick.

Now we were climbing up on the gallery steps to exchange *comment ça va*'s with our hosts. Monsieur Guidry wore an embroidered vest and a finely woven store-bought shirt, and Madame Guidry's bright green beaded dress made Maman look like a drab little sparrow in comparison.

Monsieur Guidry hadn't always been the richest man in the parish. Chance's daddy had made a lot of money in something called "speculation" on the New Orleans Cotton Exchange. Papa said when you had money, it wasn't hard to make more. But I didn't figure that would ever happen to our family.

Maman smiled at the Guidrys, but I knew she disapproved of the big new house they'd built, and of all

Monsieur Guidry's trips to New Orleans. She didn't like anything that threatened the way things had been for us French Acadians for the past hundred and fifty years, ever since the British had run our ancestors out of Canada and they'd had to carve out new homes in Louisiana. But I was so ready for something to change I could almost taste it in my dreams.

Just then the wail of a fiddle soared out over the muggy air. The sound caught at something in my chest, like when you've held your breath too long underwater. Chance and I looked at each other for a frozen moment before we turned and dashed inside.

Aunts and uncles, cousins and *parrains,* and everybody else from miles around congregated inside the big parlor, where the furniture and rugs had been removed to make room for dancing. With Chance close behind, I edged along the wall toward the raised musicians' platform in the corner where the sound was coming from.

And there he was: my uncle, 'Nonc Adolphe Olivier. He was still tall and lean and handsome, but older and more weather-beaten than I remembered. His dust-colored hair was short and curly, his mustache a trim line across his upper lip. Beside him sat Monsieur Joseph Hébert, with an accordion on his knee, and behind them was old Jean Boutté, who always beat the time on his *'ti fer,* or triangle, no matter who was playing.

As they finished a song, the last high, drawn-out fiddle notes made my scalp tingle. 'Nonc flashed a wide grin and tucked his rust-colored fiddle under his arm. The crowd, made up of just about everybody we knew, clapped and hooted wildly.

I was a little confused by all this hurrah over him. I'd been hearing nothing but Maman's gripes for so long that he'd practically turned into the boogeyman in my mind. And now everyone was treating him like Napoleon returned from exile.

'Nonc Adolphe bowed his head as the crowd kept on clapping. I was just about to call out his name when he lifted his bow again. It hovered in the air for a second, then dropped onto the strings and began to saw back and forth as if it would cut that fiddle in half.

As the rich tangle of sounds poured out into the air, the crowd quickly broke up into pairs, and the pairs began to move together in a wide circle. As if under a magic spell, everyone there seemed caught up in a whirlwind of sound. 'Nonc closed his eyes and tilted his head to the side like he was in a trance.

It was an old French song that I'd heard a million times before. But this time I heard it with more than my ears—I heard it with my whole self. The music latched onto something inside of me, as if each note was plucking a string that I hadn't even known was there. When the fiddle soared up to the high notes, I felt a quiver in my throat, and the low notes rumbled down into my belly.

And when 'Nonc opened his mouth and let out the French words in his high, mournful voice, I felt my heart flip over like a catfish on a line.

From that moment until this, that sound has never, not for one single second, let go of me. It was as if I was waking up for the first time, and I knew I could never go back to sleep.

I wished the song would never end, but at last it wound down and dropped us all to earth again. The room exploded in applause. The same breathless look shone on everybody else's face that I knew was on mine. Chance stuck his elbow in my ribs and raised his eyebrows at me.

'Nonc Adolphe's eyes swung across the crowd, stopping before they got to me. He blew a kiss to someone, and when I turned to see who it was, there stood Maman and Papa in the middle of the crowd. Maman's face was flushed, her blue eyes flashing. She gave a little nod and looked away. Papa raised his hand and waved.

The thing is, going against family is a cardinal sin among us Louisiana Cajuns. Even though they tell us we're Americans, we still speak the French of our ancestors and stick together like goslings in the nest.

"One more," said 'Nonc, "and then I got me some fences to mend." He said something to Monsieur Hébert, tucked his fiddle under his chin, and let out the first sweet notes of Maman's favorite song, *"La Valse du Bayou."* Papa held out his hand for Maman to dance, but she shook her head, turned, and made her way out to the hall. The music cast another spell over the rest of us as the room spun in a colorful blur and my insides hummed again.

Of course, no one wanted him to quit playing, but 'Nonc grinned sheepishly. "Naw, naw, you've got yourself a fiddler for the night—Moïse Thibodeaux. Come on, Moïse, I done stole your place long enough."

Moïse hurried up to the platform. He wasn't that bad a fiddler, he just wasn't that good, and hearing him next to 'Nonc Adolphe was like trying to swallow a pickle after a bowl of peach ice cream. The crowd grumbled good-naturedly as 'Nonc Adolphe put away his fiddle and stepped off the platform, practically landing on my toes.

At first 'Nonc didn't recognize me. But then he jumped back in surprise and set his fiddle case down.

"Is this—ah, no, this can't be that scrawny little fellow I used to know!" He pumped my hand and took me by the shoulders, looking me up and down. "Doggone it, Félix, you done some stretching since I saw you last. You gonna be tall like me. How old are you now?"

"You remember, 'Nonc Adolphe—I was born the same year as the twentieth century."

"Durned if you're not right. That would make you fourteen."

I nodded.

"So what you got to say for yourself, '*ti boy?*" That's what he'd always called me, "little boy." "I guess I can't call you that anymore, eh? I'll have to call you 'Stretch.'"

I was suddenly struck dumb. Nothing would come out of my mouth. Then, without even landing on the thought, I heard myself say, "Where you been, 'Nonc Adolphe, and why'd you stay away so long?" As soon as the words were out, I could've kicked myself. It was the same kind of nagging thing Maman would say.

He straightened up and looked at me with a little frown. Then his face eased up and he said, "I remember that about you, '*ti boy*—you always did ask too many questions. But that's one I better get used to answering, I guess." He rubbed his chin. "Let's just say there's a lot of roads out there, and a lot of songs to play, too. It took me a while to get around to coming back, that's all." He gave me a wink.

"So you'll be staying here from now on?" I asked.

He laughed. "Let's don't harvest the corn before it's ripe, Stretch. Now, where did that mama of yours get to? I got a feeling she's got a few questions for me, too."

Tante Mathilde, Papa's widowed sister who had the gift of healing, suddenly appeared in front of 'Nonc Adolphe. She always dressed in black from head to foot, as if her husband hadn't been dead for nearly twenty years. "Trouble rides in on a hare," she said mysteriously, shaking her finger at him, "but it rides out on a tortoise."

She was always saying strange stuff like that. Puzzled, 'Nonc looked at me. I shrugged my shoulders, and we both laughed as Tante Mathilde disappeared. Just then Chance nudged me from behind.

"Oh—you remember Chance, eh, 'Nonc?" I said.

"*Mais oui*—you're Léo's boy, ain't you?"

"Yes, sir," said Chance.

"Are you lucky like your name?" That's what the word *chance* means in French, lucky. He *was* the luckiest guy I'd ever met, with a rich daddy, a great big house, and a crazy, laughing family. And in the last year he'd grown two inches taller than me, his shoulders were wider than mine would likely ever be, and his voice had deepened. He got everything he ever wanted, and more. I'd known him since he was nearly as poor as we were, and sometimes it was hard to take.

I saw with satisfaction that Chance was as tongue-tied as I'd been. At last I had something that he didn't have— a fiddle-playing uncle who left him speechless.

I hoped 'Nonc Adolphe was here to stay.

Restless Streaks

Moïse Thibodeaux's fiddle hit a sour high note that made 'Nonc cringe. "If you boys'll excuse me, I better find that sister of mine and face a different kind of music. Stretch, you go find yourself some pretty girl to dance with."

"Naw, I don't go in much for dancing."

"Not yet you don't," said 'Nonc Adolphe, turning away. He didn't get very far, though. Men patted him on the back, and women blushed and smiled, and nobody seemed to care that he'd left Maman and Papa high and dry.

"What you think your mama's going to say to your uncle?" said Chance. When I shrugged, he whispered, "Why don't we go find out?"

I looked at him sideways. He was always one for an adventure and was forever getting me into trouble. But once he'd thought up something, I never could resist his ideas. I gave him a nod, and we tailed 'Nonc Adolphe.

Out in the hall 'Nonc approached Maman, who was looking sort of miserable among all the cheerful decorations. 'Nonc went over, took her by the elbow, and led her out onto the deep gallery that ran across the front of the house. Papa followed as they made their way to the end of the porch, through the clusters of men who'd come outside to take swigs of whiskey and talk farm prices and politics.

"C'mon," said Chance, "we can listen from my parents' room." We slipped into their big bedroom and hunkered down in the shadows by the tall window that opened onto the gallery.

"What is there to say, Adolphe?" Maman was saying, her voice tight. "You didn't even have the decency to stop by our house when you got back. We had to find you here at Léo and Alice's. What must everyone think?"

"I wanted to come home for Christmas. I just got here this afternoon, and I knew you'd be here," said 'Nonc, in the same hopeless tone I used when Maman was fussing at me.

"You could have waited for us when we arrived, so we could have a proper greeting. But no, your music came first, as always."

"Let's hear him out, Marie." That was Papa, the voice of reason.

"Thank you, André," said 'Nonc, his silhouette sharp against the purple and black sky. He cleared his throat and spread his hands in front of him. "How can I explain, Marie? You think everything in life is supposed to fall into

a straight line. But that ain't always the way it plays."
Maman folded her arms and glared.

'Nonc Adolphe peered into her eyes. "You always knew
I had a restless streak as wide as the Mississippi River. I
wasn't cut out to be a farmer." He shrugged and held his
hands out helplessly. "I tried to take up where Papa left off
when he died, I really did. But one day I woke up out there
in the field, doing the never-ending plowing and planting
and hoeing and tending in the blazing sun, and I could feel
it sucking the life right out of me."

Maman's eyes narrowed. "So you just ran off to play
your fiddle, right? Without a word of explanation." I'd
never heard such anger in her voice. "Did you ever give a
thought to us? If we'd known you didn't intend to be a
farmer, we'd never have taken on another farm—we
could've just moved back home. But no, nothing counts
to you except that fiddle of yours—" Her voice trembled
at those last words, and 'Nonc Adolphe's head drooped. I
knew just how he felt—with Maman, you had to be perfect or else.

"Calm down, Marie," said Papa, putting his arm
around her, "before you say something you can't take
back." Maman turned and hid her face in his shoulder.
"What's your plan, Adolphe, now that you're back?" said
Papa.

'Nonc Adolphe gave a bitter little laugh. "Everybody
keeps asking me that," he said. "I came back because my

conscience wouldn't quit nagging at me. I mean to give farming another shot."

Just then Monsieur Guidry stepped out onto the porch. "Food's hot!" he called. "Come and get it!"

Chance and I sneaked out of his parents' room and followed our noses to the dining room. Dodging grownups' elbows, we heaped our plates with roast beef and duck, sweet potatoes, butterbeans, rolls, and jambalaya. We headed out the back door and sat on the steps to eat.

"Your mama's plenty mad at your uncle," said Chance between bites.

"Yeah," I said, sucking on a crisp duck wing.

"He sure can play that fiddle, though," he said. "Seems like when you can do that, some of that other stuff don't matter."

"I know," I said.

For a while all I could hear was my jawbone working.

"Boy, I bet he's seen a lot of places," said Chance. "I bet New Orleans was the first place he went."

"Maybe so." I pictured that famous city over to the southeast that I'd heard Chance's daddy talk about. It sat in a crook of the mighty Mississippi River, with ships coming and going from all over the world, and musicians playing on every street corner.

Chance interrupted my reverie. "You think he'll stick around this time?"

"How should I know?"

"Well, what *do* you know?" said Chance.

"Only one thing," I said. "I know I want a piece of that chocolate cake your mama made before it's all gone."

I swung open the back door and nearly knocked over Papa.

"I suppose we could spare him for the day," he was saying to 'Nonc Adolphe, who stood behind the door. "There he is now. You can ask him yourself."

"Ask me what?" I said. Chance hovered at my elbow.

"Your papa's lending me his wagon to go to town for supplies tomorrow," said 'Nonc. "I thought maybe you'd like to go with me."

I nodded like crazy.

"I'll meet you in the morning, then. Thanks, André." 'Nonc picked up his fiddle and left, leaving behind a charged silence like the stillness between a lightning strike and a crash of thunder.

I ate my chocolate cake, followed by a thick slice of pecan pie. But once our bellies were full, and with 'Nonc Adolphe gone, the party seemed pretty dull, as if some of the color had faded out of the scene. I sat watching Moïse Thibodeaux play his fiddle but didn't feel it inside like when 'Nonc had played. So I didn't complain when Papa called me to leave.

That night as I lay in bed in the dark *garçonnière*, the

upstairs room I shared with Paulo, I thought of what 'Nonc had said to Maman. I knew just what he meant about life on the farm. I was the oldest boy, the one who was expected to carry on with the family farm. I could already plow a straight furrow, set out a sweet potato slip just right, and pick cotton as fast as anybody. Papa was proud of me, I knew.

But even in the years when the crops were good we had to plan for the years when it rained too much or too little, or when the boll weevils attacked, or when bad luck came knocking in some other way. Papa never seemed to be able to get ahead, and nothing ever happened at home but work, work, and more work. And neither Papa nor Maman seemed to mind that they'd never been beyond the parish line.

But I was different. There was a whole wide world out there that I read about in the newspapers and heard about at school, full of new inventions like aeroplanes and automobiles and railroads going places far away. If I stayed where I was, it was all going to pass me by.

Tomorrow I was going to Eunice with 'Nonc Adolphe. It wasn't New Orleans, but at least it was somewhere.

chapter three

Secrets of the Universe

I woke early the next morning and had my chores done by sunup. Then I hitched up the team to the wagon and shaded my eyes for 'Nonc Adolphe.

I couldn't believe my luck. Not only was I going to town with my famous uncle, but I was getting out of another long Saturday of working on Papa's levee, too.

Each year the bayou, which normally was a slow-moving muddy little stream, swelled with water from the spring rains and flooded our land. Each year it robbed us of more and more topsoil and drowned out anything we planted in the low acres that ran along it.

So Papa had hit upon the idea of building a levee, a tall mound of dirt, along the bayou to hold back the water. He was possessed by the idea, and we had to spend every spare moment shoveling dirt from higher ground into a wheelbarrow and dumping it onto the snaking pile. Papa was determined to finish before spring planting, and our Saturdays were spent toiling endlessly over the levee, which grew inch by slow inch.

Maman called me inside for breakfast.

"I still can't get over Adolphe," she was saying to Papa, "the way he takes the farm so lightly. As if our ancestors hadn't given their lives so he could have that privilege."

"Yeah," said Paulo, "tell us the story of the Acadians, Maman. And how come we talk French instead of English like *les Américains*."

I sighed and rolled my eyes. I'd heard this story about thirteen thousand times. Maman was never going to let us forget how our ancestors got to Louisiana and how bad they'd been treated by the British.

"Well," she said in a sad voice, "it was a long time ago, back in the 1750s. The French Acadians had lived on the east coast of Canada, a place they called *Acadie*, for a hundred and fifty years. They'd worked long and hard to build up their farms. But then England and France went to war, and *les maudits anglais*"—the blasted British—"told the Acadians they had to swear allegiance to the King of England if they wanted to stay on their own lands. And the Acadians said no."

"And then," said Paulo, taking up the tale, "the *maudits anglais* locked all the men up in a church and tried to make them sign the paper. And when they wouldn't, they burned down all their houses and loaded the people onto ships and put them out to sea."

"That's right," said Maman. "They sent them off to England or America or France, scattering families to the wind and stealing all the lands they left behind."

When I was Paulo's age, I used to wake up dreaming

that the British were burning down our house. But today I didn't want to hear all this old stuff again.

"Nearly half of the Acadians died on those boats or trying to run away from the British," Maman droned on. "Others found their way to Louisiana, where people spoke French just like they did. And here they settled and started all over again. We must never forget how our ancestors suffered, and how lucky we are to have our homes and our language and our traditions. . . ."

"And they all lived happily ever after," I thought, "and never ever went anywhere else."

The sun was halfway to noon before 'Nonc Adolphe finally appeared on his big roan stallion, Gypsy.

"Sorry, Stretch," he said. "I found me a roadhouse to play in last night where they don't know when to quit."

"Can I go to Eunice with you?" asked Paulo, appearing from nowhere. 'Nonc saw the irritation on my face. "Not this time, PeeWee," he said.

Paulo's face drooped as we pulled the wagon onto the road, with Gypsy tied behind.

A Saturday in Eunice, ten miles away, was always an adventure. The muddy streets were crammed with wagons, buggies, livestock, and even the occasional automobile. Children ran up and down the wooden sidewalks, and neighbors clustered to catch up on news and gossip.

At the general mercantile we loaded up on flour, sugar, coffee, cornmeal, and other staples, and 'Nonc Adolphe also bought lumber, nails, whitewash, and paint. "The old house is getting pretty shabby," he explained. "I better get to work on it now, while there's not much fieldwork to be done. Come spring planting, I'll be a slave to the plow again."

I nodded, thinking how happy Maman would be to hear that.

"Now I've got another stop to make," said 'Nonc. I trailed him down the street and through the big glass doors of Ardoin's Emporium.

Ardoin's was the fanciest store in town, and I'd never set foot in it before. The wood floors gleamed and electric lights glinted from the ceiling. The smells of fancy perfumes and new leather followed us up a massive staircase to the second floor.

'Nonc strode through the furniture department and the sporting goods toward a display of trumpets and horns and accordions. And there, behind the counter like a regiment of soldiers at attention, stood two rows of fiddles.

I stared at them in awe. Their curved lines shone in different colored varnishes, and they beckoned to me like cotton to a boll weevil.

"You like 'em?" said 'Nonc.

I nodded.

"Then let's try one out."

"Not me," I said timidly. "You go on."

A tall, skinny sales clerk appeared, wearing little round glasses and a badge that read AMOS VOORHIES. "May I help you?" he said, sounding as if his glasses were pinching his nose.

"We'd like to take a look at your fiddles."

"Very good, sir," said Amos Voorhies. "What price range were you interested in?"

"My friend," said 'Nonc, "it's the quality that counts. Let's try that one on the end."

Over the top of his glasses, the clerk sized up 'Nonc. "Very good, sir." He pulled down the fiddle and handed it over the counter. "Each of our better violins comes with this handsome case, fully lined in felt, with a cake of the finest rosin and a complete instruction book that makes it easy to learn to play."

"You don't say?" said 'Nonc Adolphe, playing a few notes. He quickly handed it back and tried the next one. He liked it better and played awhile on it before trading it for the next one.

Nearby a little girl pulled her mother over to listen to the music. A farmer in overalls started to clap his hands. Pretty soon a small crowd of people had gathered around us, tapping their feet and smiling. Wherever he went, it seemed people followed 'Nonc like cows to the milking.

Mr. Voorhies was getting impatient, but 'Nonc didn't seem to notice and just kept trading fiddles. Each one of them had a different sound, the way no two people's voices are alike. Some were low and deep, some were shrill, some were mellow and some loud.

A man stepped up and put two dimes in the fiddle case on the counter. "Play us a waltz, *mon ami*," he said.

'Nonc Adolphe flashed him a smile and ran through a slow waltz. I felt the same response as the night before, like the music was vibrating on the inside of me.

"A contredanse," said another man, tossing in another quarter. People kept putting money into the case, and 'Nonc kept on playing. Every once in a while he would trade fiddles, then start right back up again. Feet were tapping and heads were bobbing as the notes poured out like water from a spring.

I watched the clerk's face get redder and redder until the veins stood out on his forehead. At last he came around the counter and planted himself in front of 'Nonc Adolphe. "Now, see here," he said in his pinched voice, "this is not a dance hall. Please move along, move along." As his audience left, 'Nonc stopped playing and picked up the money from the case, stuffing it into his coat pocket.

Mr. Voorhies watched in shocked silence. "Which of the instruments were you interested in?" he stammered.

"Oh, I think I'll keep the one I have," said 'Nonc. "I really just need a new set of strings."

Mr. Voorhies's nose went up as if he smelled something rotten. "Very well, sir," he said, meaning just the opposite. 'Nonc paid for the strings out of the money from the crowd and, with a *merci beaucoup,* turned on his heel and walked away.

I barely made it outside before I burst out laughing. "You sure had him going, 'Nonc Adolphe! How much money did you make?"

"Enough to buy us lunch at Myer's," said 'Nonc with a grin.

I'd never eaten in a restaurant before. I followed 'Nonc into the lobby of Myer's Hotel, then on into the restaurant. Every table sported a white tablecloth, a vase of flowers, and white dishes with gold rims. I felt out of place in my homespun trousers and shirt, but 'Nonc walked in like he owned the place.

A man in a black suit led us to a table by the window and handed us a menu.

I ordered pork chops with rice and gravy, some fancy carrots, and the fluffiest white rolls I'd ever seen. I wanted to pinch myself. There I was, eating lunch in a restaurant with 'Nonc Adolphe, who'd seen the world.

Through mouthfuls of food, I asked, "Did you ever ride in an automobile?" He nodded. "What's it feel like?"

"Like you're riding on a goose-down pillow."

I tried to imagine that. "What's the best place you've ever been to?"

"That would have to be New Orleans. It's like no other place in the world," said 'Nonc. "The buildings look like they're trimmed in lace. That Creole food is the best in the world. The music doesn't stop until the sun comes up, and the ladies are the prettiest you'll find anywhere on the continent." He winked and leaned back in his chair.

"Someday I'm going there," I said. "If I ever get off the farm."

"There's nothing wrong with the farm," said 'Nonc.

"But it's the same old thing every year," I said. "The only thing that changes is how bad the weather is." The waiter put a fat piece of pecan pie in front of me. "Besides, I heard what you told Maman last night. Why, she's never been any farther in her whole life than right here in Eunice."

"Maybe she doesn't want to go anywhere else," said 'Nonc.

"Well, I do."

The sun had sunk low in the western sky by the time we pulled up in front of 'Nonc Adolphe's house. It was a big house, compared to ours, built of good swamp cypress by my great-great-grandfather before the War Between the States. But now the proud old house seemed to hunker down on itself in the deep gloom of its gallery. The white paint was peeling off the walls, a wisteria vine had taken over the front door, and the steps were sagging and rotten.

Out back, surrounded by a rusty iron fence, were all

the graves of Maman's parents and grandparents and great-grandparents. Land to a Cajun is the most important thing there is, and once he has it, he never lets it go.

I stood there a minute, feeling the struggles of my ancestors in the soil under my feet. It occurred to me how stubborn they had been and how they gave up everything rather than let somebody else boss them around. I knew the same stubbornness was alive and well in me.

Inside, everything was covered in a thick coat of grime, and dust motes danced in the late-afternoon light. "I've got my work cut out for me," said 'Nonc Adolphe sheepishly.

"I'll say." We started unloading the sacks and cartons from the wagon. Each time I passed through the living room, 'Nonc's fiddle case on the table pulled at me like a magnet, until on one trip I found myself alone in the room. Glancing over my shoulder, I unlatched the little peg from the leather loop that held it closed. There it lay, as if in a dream—a real fiddle.

"Go on, give it a try," said 'Nonc from the doorway, making me jump.

"Really?"

"Sure. You ain't gonna break it." He came over, lifted my head, and stuck the fiddle on my shoulder, then pressed my chin down on top of it. "You hold it with the weight of your head. Then take the bow like this"—he wrapped the fingers of my right hand around the end of the stick—"and you pull it across the strings."

I did. It sounded like a billy goat in misery.

"Press a little harder," said 'Nonc. When I did, it sounded like a howling cat. 'Nonc threw back his head and laughed, and I felt my face flush red.

"Aw, don't take it so serious," said 'Nonc, slapping me on the back. "You sound better than I did the first time I tried it. Turn around here and let me give you a hand." He spun me around and stood behind me, holding the bow along with me. "You got to dig into those strings, just like you dig into life. If you don't, you'll just skim along the surface and miss all the good stuff."

He pressed down on the bow, drawing it down and back up, and the sound I'd been hearing in my head came out.

"Now you. Try and stay on one string at a time."

I pressed into a string with the bow, and sure enough, it sounded good. "That's it," said 'Nonc. "Now try another string. Right. Keep going. Now put a finger down."

When I did, the sound went higher. I lifted my finger and the sound went lower. I tried it on another string, and another. Sheer joy rose up my gullet, like I'd been let in on a secret of the universe.

"That's your E-string," said 'Nonc, pointing to the skinny string on the right. "The next one down is an A, then a D, and a G. The names of the notes are letters, just like the alphabet. The strings are tuned four notes apart from each other, so you've got three fingers to fill in the notes in between."

I got up my courage to press the strings with a second finger and then a third, meanwhile drawing the bow back and forth faster and faster over the strings, trying to look like 'Nonc when he played. He roared with laughter.

"Not bad, '*ti boy*," said 'Nonc. "You're an Olivier, all right. I suppose it's in your blood, too. Let me show you something I found up in the attic." He disappeared into the bedroom and returned with a faded old daguerreotype in a frame. He held it out to me.

A man in an old-fashioned suit stood stiffly in front of flowered wallpaper, with a fiddle held under his arm and a bow dangling from his hand. "Who's this?"

"Why, that's your grandpapa, Octave Olivier," said 'Nonc. "That's where you got your middle name. He died when you were a *petit bébé*."

My heart stopped.

"He was a handsome devil, don't you think?" said 'Nonc. "Matter of fact, when I first saw you the other night, I noticed how much you look like him."

"He was a fiddler?" I stammered. "I thought he was a farmer." Maman talked about her daddy all the time, but she'd never mentioned this one crucial fact.

"Some people can do both, unless they're crazy in the head like me." 'Nonc stared thoughtfully at the picture. "Oh, Papa loved his music. He used to sit out there on the gallery and play every day at sundown. Always said he was putting the sun to bed."

"How come nobody ever told me that?"

"I don't know. More'n likely, your mama didn't want to put any ideas into your head. She don't take to fiddlers, in case you haven't noticed."

"I've noticed."

"That's mostly my fault—she blames my fiddle for my wandering ways. But the truth is, that's just how I'm made." He sighed. "But now it's time to mend my ways."

I peered into my grandfather's eyes. They were large and dark like mine, and the corners wanted to turn up even in the stiff pose. "He's the one who taught me to play the fiddle," said 'Nonc.

"Is that the same fiddle you play?"

"You better believe—the one and only. The story goes that he bought it off a peddler that came through one day, way back before he married your grandma. The peddler claimed it came from the Opera House down in New Orleans." 'Nonc picked up his fiddle and held it as gently as a newborn baby. "It's got a better tone than anything I heard in that store today, that's for sure. That reminds me, I want to put those new strings on."

I followed him outside and sat beside him on the rickety gallery steps. He began to twist a peg, which loosened a string. He tossed the old string out and threaded a new one in its place.

I watched, fascinated by the process. At last I took a deep breath. "'Nonc, you think you could teach me to play the fiddle?"

'Nonc stared me in the face for a moment before saying, "There's nothing I'd like better, Stretch." My heart jumped out of my throat. "But I can't." My stomach bottomed out.

"Why not?"

"Because your mama wouldn't allow it. I came home to make peace with her, and that's what I'm going to do. Besides, a musician's life ain't easy."

"What do you mean?"

"I mean it's lonesome, that's what."

"Lonesome? Why, you must be the most popular man in the state! And all those places you've been . . ."

"I've been places 'cause I had to keep moving to make a living. I never had a place to call home in all the time I was gone."

Desperation rose through my chest. "What if Maman said it was all right for you to teach me?"

"Not much chance of that," said 'Nonc, twisting pegs and plucking strings into tune. "But I guess it wouldn't hurt to ask. If she says it's OK, then your wish is my command."

I snapped the reins, and the surprised horses trotted through the deepening twilight. The wind had changed to the north, and black thunderclouds roiled in the distance. I unhitched, brushed, and fed and watered the team in a daze, barely knowing what I was doing.

The lamps were lit in the kitchen, throwing beacons of light into the gloom as I hurried in for supper. I had to tell about my trip in detail. Meanwhile my big question swelled in my throat, threatening to explode.

At last, as Maman began to clear the table, I found the right moment. As nonchalantly as possible, I said, "Oh, I almost forgot. 'Nonc showed me how you hold a fiddle. He said he wouldn't mind teaching me how to play."

For a moment silence reigned. Then the dishes clattered back onto the table. Maman's voice was deep and fierce as she said, "Félix Octave LeBlanc, you will not play the fiddle as long as there is breath in my body. You are forbidden to even *say* that word again in this house, do you understand?"

My mouth dropped open. "What's so bad about it? And how come you never even told me my grandpapa was a fiddler?"

Maman drew herself up like a cat ready to pounce. "I knew Adolphe would be a bad influence on you. Here he is, back one day and already he's turning your head."

"He hasn't turned my head, Maman. . . ."

"If you think for one minute you're going to end up like that lazy, shiftless, no-good brother of mine, you need to think again."

"But, Maman, he's not as bad as you think. . . ."

"Félix," said Papa. "You heard your mother."

"But it's not fair!" My voice rose to a shout. "It's in my blood!"

"Don't you use that tone of voice with me. Go to your room, young man," said Maman.

The injustice of it all welled up inside me till I could hardly see. If I said anything else, I would explode. I stood up, knocking my chair over behind me, and stormed away.

"I'll find a way, and you can't stop me," I muttered under my breath. "I'm going to be a fiddler."

Square Roots

Raindrops splattered on the roof as I lay on my bed. Staring at me from the walls were all the pictures I'd torn from the Sears and Roebuck mail-order catalogues of things I dreamed of having—a twelve-gauge shotgun, a bicycle, a talking machine that would play music any time you wanted. I had no chance in Hades of getting a single one of them.

I heard steps on the stairs. It was Papa, coming to sit beside me on the bed.

Expecting a harsh talking-to, I was surprised to hear him say, "It's not easy being fourteen, is it, son?" I stared at the ceiling.

"I remember when I was your age," he went on. "Sometimes it felt like I'd never grow up and do all the things I wanted. Like there was red pepper in my blood, making me itch from the inside."

I looked at him, surprised to hear him describe exactly what I was feeling.

"But you know what I've learned since then?" he said.

I shook my head. "That the years you're living now are some of the very best ones of your life. 'Cause it won't be long till you start feeling the weight of responsibility, and that can get mighty heavy at times."

Papa's shoulders sagged from endless hard work, and the furrows in his face got deeper every year. But it was hard to imagine that this was as good as my life was going to get. "What does that have to do with me learning to fiddle?"

He tapped his fingertips together. "I don't blame you for being charmed by Adolphe," he said. "He's the best musician I've ever known. But he's irresponsible—always running off, leaving things undone, staying out all hours of the night. It doesn't make for a good reputation. Not to mention all the trouble he's caused us."

"OK, Papa, that's 'Nonc Adolphe," I said. "But Grandpapa wasn't like that, and he played the fiddle. I'm talking about *me*. You know I'd never run off and leave you high and dry."

"You're a good boy, Félix," said Papa, "and you've always made us proud. But your mother feels too strongly about this, and you're not going to change her mind. You'll understand it better when you're older. Besides, we don't have a spare cent for buying fiddles. So I'm sorry, but that's final." He waited for me to answer. "Félix?"

"Yes, sir," I said, as if there were slivers of glass in my mouth.

"Goodnight, then." Papa got up and left me to my misery.

Rain pounded the roof all night long, banging the shutters and dripping through the cypress shingles in the usual spots. Paulo snored through it all, but I tossed in my bed like a boat off its moorings.

The sheets chafed my skin. The echoes of 'Nonc Adolphe's songs rang loud in my ears. I felt a smoldering in my chest, as if I'd swallowed something too hot that got stuck in my craw. My cheeks burned, too, and my fingers drummed a rhythm on the homespun blanket. I woke feeling like I hadn't slept in years.

Maman hurried us through breakfast so we'd make it to Mass on time. We bundled up against the cold weather that had arrived with the storm, loaded up in the wagon, and headed for town.

The little town of L'Anse Rougeau was built at a crossroads of the east-west and north-south roads. It was made up of the Catholic church, our one-room schoolhouse, Monsieur Adam Vidrine's store, and a couple of dozen houses. Chance waved at me as we took our usual pew, and I gave him a miserable wave back. As Père Benoît droned on about the lessons of Christmas, I did what I usually did—found a quiet place inside myself where I could dream.

Sometimes I pretended I was Calbraith P. Rodgers,

flying an aeroplane clear across the United States. Sometimes I was Ty Cobb coming up to bat, trying to break one of my own baseball records. And sometimes I was a French infantryman, fighting off the Germans in the trenches over in Europe.

But today, in my mind, I went straight to a raised platform in the corner of Chance's parlor, put a red fiddle under my chin, and sawed away on it with a bow until magic music came pouring out. It was a dream that wouldn't go away.

As we sloshed along the muddy road home, I looked at my family, the two grownups on the wagon seat, the two kids in back. Maman had lost three babies in between Paulo and me; they were all buried behind 'Nonc Adolphe's house. So instead of a big family like most Cajuns had, there were just the four of us, like the sides of a plain old square. Maybe that was why Maman hovered over us like a protective mother hen.

I had Papa's wiry brown hair and dark eyes, but was tall like Maman's side of the family. Now Paulo, he had Maman's straight black hair and blue eyes, but he was built just like Papa, short and stocky.

In the distance sat our square house, with the steep roof that all Acadian houses had, and a deep gallery across the front, with the outside stairs leading up to the room Paulo and I shared. Downstairs the square was divided into two rooms, one a combination kitchen and living room, and the other my parents' bedroom, with a tiny room off the back gallery for Maman's loom. In the harsh light of midday, our place looked small and drab.

Sunday dinner was the same old roast chicken and rice dressing we always had. I barely tasted it, engrossed in the echoes of the last couple of days and the pictures that flashed endlessly before my eyes.

It was one of those pictures that brought an unexpected ray of hope—the Sears and Roebuck mail-order catalogue! I was sure I'd seen musical instruments in it. The minutes crawled by until the dishes were cleared and everyone went off to enjoy the one day of rest of the week. I snatched the "Wish Book," as we called it, since we wished for so many things out of it, from its place of honor beside the fireplace, and headed outside.

"Where you goin', Félix?" asked Paulo, appearing out of thin air. He was always following me around like a flop-eared puppy, and lately it rubbed on my nerves like coarse-grit sandpaper.

"None of your beeswax," I answered.

"You don't fool me—you're going up to the barn loft, just like you always do."

"And you're not," I said, slamming the door behind me. I headed into the barn and up the ladder to the loft, where I kept some hay bales stacked in an out-of-the-way corner in the shape of a chair. I called it my "throne," and it was where I did my best thinking and reading and day-dreaming.

Sinking into the sweet-smelling hay, I held my breath and thumbed to the musical goods. And there they were—five whole pages of fiddles.

My eyes drank in the pictures like cold lemonade on a hot day. Just the shape of the instrument was beautiful, the way it curved here and there and pulled in at the middle. Then there was the long neck that held the strings, and the fancy wood scroll at the end of that. I could almost feel the weight of the thing in my hands.

I held the book to the light and puzzled out the English words. There were Maggini models and Stradivarius and Paganini and Guarnerius models, and other foreign and exotic names.

Some of them were made of silver or Cremona spruce, and some of curled or flamed maple. Some had real ebony tailpieces and fingerboards inlaid with mother-of-pearl. Some came with a case, a bow, a finger chart, extra strings, and a box of rosin to rub on the strings, which made me remember the white powder flying off 'Nonc Adolphe's fiddle when he played.

And then came the best part. Under a picture of a man in a fancy suit playing a violin, I read, *"To learn is easy—it's just a question of getting started. The earning capacity of a proficient violinist often exceeds $100.00 per week!"* Why, with that kind of money I could go anywhere in the world.

There was one small problem. The cheapest fiddle in the book cost $2.65, and they ran all the way up to the "Concert Model" at $27.95!

Before I could make money, I'd need to spend some. And I didn't have a prayer of coming up with enough.

At breakfast the next morning Maman acted like nothing had happened. "Félix," she said, "I need some thread from the store to finish your winter shirts. Will you go by after school and get me two large spools of dark brown? Here's a dime."

"Yes, ma'am. C'mon, Paulo," I said, running out into the chill morning air to bridle Henri, the old swaybacked mule we rode to school. Sticking our lunch pails into an old pair of saddlebags slung over the mule's rump, I jumped on his back and pulled Paulo up after me. My breath blew white and my ears stung with the cold as Henri trudged the two miles to school.

Grades one through nine shared the same schoolroom under the eagle eye of Mademoiselle Sonnier. She was an old maid, gnarled like an ancient live oak, and she'd rap your knuckles with a ruler as soon as look at you. Chance tumbled in just as she rang the bell and joined us older kids in the back of the room.

I tried to keep my mind on my work, but it kept drifting back to the pictures in the catalogue, to the weight of 'Nonc's fiddle resting on my shoulder, to the feelings that the music brought to life inside of me. So when Mademoiselle called on me to answer a sum, she might as well have asked me to name the pharaohs of Egypt. She gave me a scorching look and suggested I pay attention.

It was my turn to tend the fire at lunchtime, so I didn't get to talk to Chance. The day dragged on, but at last the big brass bell rang dismissal. Chance followed me out the door, saying, "So what happened when you went to town with your uncle on Saturday?"

I told him about the scene at Ardoin's Emporium, our lunch at Myer's, and getting to play 'Nonc's fiddle.

Chance punched my arm. "He showed you how to play it?" he asked incredulously.

"Well, he showed me how to hold it, and how to play a couple of notes." I basked for a moment in Chance's envy before recalling Maman's words the other night. "I'm going by the store," I said dejectedly. "Want to come?"

"Sure, I'll go with you and get a pop," said Chance, mounting his gray-spotted Appaloosa mare, Cherokee.

Deciding not to embarrass poor old Henri by riding him alongside Cherokee, I tugged on his reins to walk him to the store, with Paulo trailing behind. As I tied up under the "Cheap for Cash" sign at the store, Chance swung his leg over the big Appaloosa's back and headed straight for the soda box by the door, pulling a nickel from the never-ending supply in his pocket. "Want one?" he said.

"No thanks," I said. I had my pride.

Chance pulled a red soda out of the box, knocked the top off, and tilted his head back. My mouth watered as the *pop rouge* disappeared. "See you tomorrow," he said, and cantered away.

As I said, he was a lucky guy.

Paulo and I stepped inside, letting the door slam behind us. My nostrils tingled with the smells of coffee, pickles, spices, and kerosene. Monsieur Vidrine, the store owner, appeared from the back room and made his way through the farm implements and sacks of grain that crowded the floor. Paulo headed for the toy shelf.

"Well, looka here," said Monsieur Vidrine, "if it ain't André LeBlanc's boys. What you know good, Félix?" His bald head shone in the dim light.

"Not much, Monsieur. Maman sent me in for some thread."

"Right over here," he said, making his way to the dry goods counter, where colorful bolts of fabric gleamed from the shelves. "How many spools you need?"

"Two brown ones, please."

"You got it. Hey, how'd you like that dance at the Guidrys'?" he said. "That uncle of yours sure can tickle them fiddle strings. I ain't heard the like since he's been gone!"

"Yes, sir," I said.

"Well, you don't sound none too happy about it to me."

Something about his smiling face made me say, "It's just that I was hoping I'd get to learn to play the fiddle myself. But Maman doesn't want me being a fiddler, and Papa says we can't afford to buy a fiddle anyway."

"Hmm," said Monsieur Vidrine, shaking his head. "I know how you feel. Now, me, I always wanted to learn to play the accordion. I could just see myself playing at the dance, with all the pretty girls watching and wishing they could dance with me. We even had an old accordion that somebody gave my papa. But I never had no talent."

"At least you had your chance." I heaved a sigh.

"But you, seeing how it runs in the family, you could probably learn easy. I can remember your grandpapa playing at the dances when I was a boy." He peered into my face. "You know, come to think of it, you favor him a good bit." He wrapped the thread in brown paper and tied it with twine as if sealing my fate.

But then he leaned over the counter and said thoughtfully, "You know, when I was a boy, I knew a fellow who made his own fiddle. Out of a cigar box. You ever think of that?"

I couldn't answer for the blood rushing in my ears.

Monsieur Vidrine rubbed his chin. "It was my buddy Philip Trahan. He took an old wooden cigar box, and carved all the other parts he needed and put them together. It didn't sound half bad, either."

"You mean it really worked?"

He nodded.

"What'd he use for a bow?"

"I think he used a stick strung up with lots of sewing thread."

My insides turned to jelly.

"Ever since I heard your uncle the other night," Monsieur Vidrine went on, looking off into the distance, "I've been thinking how there's nothing better than a good two-step to make you feel alive, and nothing like a sweet waltz to make you understand what love is all about. We all need that."

"Yes, sir," I said. "Y-y-you wouldn't have a cigar box, would you?"

"Hmm." Monsieur Vidrine took a long look at me. "Let me see what I can find," he said, and disappeared into the back. I patted my pocket where I kept my greatest treasure on earth, the two-bladed bone-handled jackknife I'd gotten for Christmas the year before. It was my only store-bought possession, and I'd whittled many a stick of wood into toys or figures with it. Maybe, just maybe, all that experience would come in handy.

I held my breath until Monsieur Vidrine appeared again, blowing a cloud of dust off a small wooden box. My cheeks pulled on the sides of my mouth.

"This ought to do you," he said. I caught a gleam in his eye as he leaned over the counter and handed it to me.

"Whatever it is you plan to do with it, do a good job, and let me see it when you're done. But don't tell your mama it was me who gave you the idea."

"A cottonmouth moccasin couldn't get it out of me," I said, grinning like a fool.

"You better check and make sure it's empty."

I opened the hinged lid. Inside were two sticks of peppermint candy. "A little *lagniappe*—something extra for good luck," said Monsieur Vidrine.

"Thanks," I said, feeling like I could hug him. Calling to Paulo, I hurried to stuff the box into the saddlebag under my lunch tin. We headed down the road toward home, my stomach turning more somersaults than a high-wire acrobat.

Dreams and Schemes

In a few minutes' ride, Paulo and I were out on the broad prairie that stretched as far as you could see, broken only by an occasional clump of hardwood forest and the trees that snaked along the coulees and the bayous. My cold fingers gripped the reins as Henri's hooves glopped through the frosty mud.

"What'd you get from Monsieur Vidrine?" Paulo's voice behind me made me jump.

I started to say it was none of his business. But I decided I might need him on my side, so I pulled out the cigar box and opened it. "M'sieur Vidrine gave us some peppermint sticks." Their crisp smell tickled my nose. I handed him one, which went straight into his mouth.

"What you gonna do with the box?"

"Nothing. I mean, it's a surprise, so you can't say anything to Maman about it."

"I won't if you give me that other stick of candy."

For a seven-year-old he was a smart little rat. I handed over the peppermint stick, then had to listen to him slurping it the rest of the way home.

I dashed upstairs to hide the contraband cigar box under the mattress, then back downstairs to hear Maman's usual "How was school today?" As I crumbled leftover corn-bread into my buttermilk, I wished I could tell her about the new world of hope that Monsieur Vidrine had just given me. But I couldn't even look her in the eye, because I knew how mad she'd be if she found out.

Just as the warmth of the kitchen began to seep into my fingertips, Maman said, "Félix, it's been so cold today that I've used up all the wood in the woodbox. You'll need to split some more before you start the milking. And get me the last of the turnips from the garden. It's liable to freeze tonight."

"Yes, ma'am," I answered, giving her a salute when she turned her back. I waited till she left the room to grab the Wish Book and rip out the pages of violins, which I stuffed into my overalls.

I pulled turnips, split wood, slopped the hogs, and milked Caillette, the cold seeping into my bones. Then, shivering, I dashed into the barn and made my way through the chilly gloom to the pile of scrap lumber in the back.

Rooting through the pieces, I soon found the perfect chunk of cypress for a fiddle neck—about ten inches long and two inches square.

"Félix! Time to eat!" called Maman. My heart pound-ing, I made another run upstairs to the *garçonnière* to stash the wood and the Sears pages under my mattress. They left a telltale lump, but I didn't have time to figure out anything else before hurrying downstairs for supper.

At bedtime I blew out the candle between our beds and lay stiff as a corpse, pretending to be asleep for Paulo's benefit. The lump of the cigar box dug into my back like a torture device, and my sweaty fingers clenched my jack-knife. Fear, mixed with excitement, made my heart pound so loud I was sure everyone could hear.

Just when I thought he had dropped off, Paulo's voice rose out of the darkness. "Félix?"

"What?" I couldn't keep the impatience out of my voice.

"What're you gonna do with that cigar box and that piece of wood under your mattress?"

My blood began a slow boil. But if I wasn't careful, he'd tell on me, and my whole plan would be shot. "I told you, it's a surprise," I said, keeping my voice calm.

"For who?"

"I can't tell you."

"Is it for me? For Christmas?"

"Maybe," I lied. Might as well pile up the sins, I thought.

Paulo yawned. "I like it when you make me stuff."

I thought of the peashooter that I was often the target of. "I'll make you something you'll like," I said, having no idea what that might be.

"OK." He rolled over and was soon taking long slow breaths.

"Paulo?" I whispered into the dark. No answer.

Swinging my feet onto the cold floor, I sat up and lit the candle on the table. My shadow loomed over me on the wall as the cigar box and the chunk of cypress emerged from my bed. I laid the pictures of the fiddles beside them.

Compared to the curvy lines of a real violin, my cigar box looked mighty square and primitive. There was nothing to be done about that, but I could make the neck more like the real thing. At the end of it, I would carve a shape like a spiraling snail shell, just like a real fiddle. In order to have enough thickness at the end for it, though, I was going to have to whittle down over half the depth of the wood.

First I used the tip of the small blade of my knife to scratch a rough outline of the shape I needed. Then I switched to the larger blade. As I touched it to the block of wood and drew it toward me, a thin shaving curled up and dropped to the floor. Another fell on top of it, and another.

My heart slammed against my chest. I was on my way.

By the time my eyelids had drooped once too often, a good-size pile of shavings lay on the floor. Half asleep, I stashed the pieces under my bed, then cut a little slit in the seam of my mattress and stuffed the shavings in among the dried Spanish moss.

It felt like I'd just blown out the candle when Maman

was shaking me awake saying I'd be late for school. My eyes popped open, and I checked for any telltale signs of my work before I staggered downstairs for breakfast and the trek to school.

That night I followed the same routine, waiting out Paulo's bedtime prattle until he fell asleep. I had to pinch myself to keep from dropping off. But after he was snoring softly and the candlelight flickered on the walls, I pulled out my treasures.

My knife touched the wood, and I watched another pile of shavings slide through my cold fingers to the floor.

As work on the fiddle neck progressed, my life began to revolve around those hours in the dead of night when I watched the wood taking shape in my hands. Somewhere along the way I stopped fretting over what would happen. Every night when my knife bit into the cypress for the first time, a feeling of peace would settle over me, and my worries would slip away.

But by Friday I was stumbling through the school day like a zombie, and I dozed off during reading. My book dropped to the floor and jolted me awake.

"Are we boring you, Monsieur LeBlanc?" asked Mademoiselle Sonnier.

"No, ma'am," I said.

"Perhaps it will help if you take the next turn to read aloud."

I struggled through two whole pages before she let me quit.

At lunch Chance said, "Hey, let's go squirrel hunting this afternoon. I'll let you borrow my shotgun."

I winced. Chance had had a shotgun ever since he was old enough to ask for one, and I still didn't have my own gun. Why, if he decided he wanted a fiddle, his daddy would probably run straight into town and buy him one. So after I'd thought about it long and hard, I'd finally decided not to tell Chance about making my fiddle just yet. That way, if it didn't turn out, I wouldn't look like such a fool.

"Naw," I said. "It's our turn to do the *boucherie* tomorrow, and I've got to help Papa get ready." Papa's brothers took turns butchering a hog and sharing the meat.

"Is your 'Nonc Adolphe coming to the *boucherie?*" asked Chance eagerly.

"I don't know," I said, shrugging, knowing full well he was. Chance was waiting for me to invite him, but I was hoping to talk to 'Nonc about my fiddle, and besides, I just didn't feel like sharing him. And the Guidrys were so rich they didn't even butcher their own meat anymore. Chance turned away dejectedly.

That night I was so exhausted I fell asleep trying to wait out Paulo, which put me a day behind in my plans. But in that first week, I'd whittled what would pass for a fiddle neck, thicker at the end where it would attach to the cigar box, and roughly rounded at the other end, where I would carve the spiral. But I still had my doubts about how well it would all work.

"Old Porker's turned into a fine, fat hog," said Papa over an early breakfast. I scooped more butter onto my grits. "Those brothers of mine will be eager to get their share of him. We'd better get to work."

I nodded, still groggy from all the sleep I'd missed.

"Give that boy another cup of coffee, Marie," said Papa. "He's got growing pains this morning."

Maman poured black coffee into my cup, and I spooned in some sugar. I felt better after that second cup, and ran upstairs to dress. The morning light spilled in the window, and I couldn't resist pulling my handiwork out from under the mattress. Holding the neck in the sunshine, I turned it round and round, watching the play of the grain in the honey-colored wood. I laid it on my collarbone and pretended to rub a bow over it with my right hand.

I still had a long way to go. But what I was holding in my hands was no longer a squared-off chunk of wood. It was the neck of a fiddle.

"Félix!" called Papa.

"Coming!" I stuffed the pieces under my bed and ran downstairs and out into the fresh December air.

༄

The sky was so blue it almost hurt your eyes. Overhead a hawk swooped and turned and spiraled like the scroll on my fiddle neck.

We'd already killed and bled the hog by the time all my uncles, aunts, and cousins arrived. I kept an eager eye out for 'Nonc Adolphe, who'd told Papa he'd be there. After the hide had been skinned and scraped, Papa and 'Nonc Louis set about butchering the hog, divvying up the choicest cuts of meat among the families.

Nothing would go to waste. The fat would be rendered for lard, and the head boiled and seasoned into hogshead cheese. The intestines would be cleaned and stuffed with ground meat and rice for *boudin,* the stomach stuffed with seasoned meat and cooked, and the lean backbone made into my favorite stew. We Cajuns had a reputation for being able to make something out of nothing, and for stretching what we had to the outer limits.

While the grownups broke up into little groups to work on their assigned tasks, my cousins and I hovered around the hot kettle where the *gratons,* or cracklings, were being fried. The hog skin had already been cut into small pieces with a little fat left on, and when it was fried, it made the crunchiest snacks you ever tasted.

I was just tossing the first hot one from hand to hand when I spied a familiar roan stallion pulling into the yard. There, sure enough, were 'Nonc Adolphe and his fiddle. Nearby the grownups' tongues started wagging.

"Look who's here," said 'Nonc Louis. "He shows up to eat after the work's been done."

"Cutting off a mule's ears won't make him a horse," said Tante Mathilde.

I looked around in time to see Maman's cheeks redden at this talk about her brother here among Papa's hard-working family.

'Nonc strode up on his long, bowed legs. "Hey, Stretch," he called to me, catching the *graton* that I tossed his way. As he began the round of kisses and *comment ça va*'s, I watched him snag one of the first links of *boudin* to come out of the sausage stuffer and make everyone laugh with a "They sure don't make this stuff in Texas!" It seemed he could work his charm on folks in spite of themselves.

When he went to the pump for a drink, I scampered after him. "She said no, 'Nonc," I whispered urgently, "just like you said she would."

He stared at me for a minute. "Oh, you mean your mama, about the fiddle. I told you so, Stretch." He stuck his hands under the water and splashed his face.

"In fact, she told me never even to say the word again."

"I'd say that's pretty final. I'm sorry, *'ti boy*. Maybe when you get older . . ."

"But I can't wait that long. I got me a cigar box, and

I'm trying to make a fiddle out of it. I've already got most of the neck carved—"

"Whoa," said 'Nonc Adolphe, holding up his hands. "I don't want to know nothing about it." He glanced over at Maman, who was watching us suspiciously. "I can't afford for that sister of mine to blame me for turning you down the wrong road. If you're bound and determined, that's your business. But count me out." And he walked away.

I stood there, my cheeks stinging as if he'd slapped me. *Wait till you get older.* Grownups just said stuff like that to keep you from having any fun. 'Nonc Adolphe had acted like he was on my side, but when the going got rough, he went along with the rest of them.

After we'd eaten the backbone stew and polished off most of the *boudin* and *gratons,* the grownups sat around a big bonfire and we kids ran off to play kickball. I heard Tante Mathilde say, "Adolphe, it's time you sang for your supper. Break out that fiddle of yours—my heels need some kicking."

I was still mad at him and wouldn't have spoken to him for a hundred dollars. But when he sat on a thick stump and pulled his fiddle out of its beat-up case, a team of mules couldn't have dragged me away. I forgot everything but watching his fingers on the strings, and listening to the sounds that came out. I sat on the ground nearby, trying to drill the music into my brain so that, when I finally got the chance, I could make those sounds come out of me and my fiddle.

The sun was long gone when everyone loaded up and went home. By then I'd learned a lot just by studying 'Nonc's playing.

If they thought I would give up that easily, they were all wrong. I wasn't a stubborn Cajun for nothing. That red pepper in my veins was burning hotter than ever to make music.

Joyeux Noël

That night I started on the scroll at the end of the neck, which they also called the head of the fiddle. Funny how it sounded like you were talking about the parts of a person, or like parts of yourself.

The scroll would be the hardest part, but I was determined to do myself proud. After studying the pictures from the catalogue, I scratched a circle inside a circle inside a circle, each connecting like the turns of a snail's shell. The challenge was to make each smaller one stand out from the larger one before it, till the smallest circle would stick out of the center. I wasn't sure I could pull it off, but I would do my best.

Starting in the center, I began making tiny cuts, shaving off a smidgen of wood with each stroke. Once or twice I shaved off a smidgen of skin, too, when the knife slipped and jabbed into my palm. But I went right on cutting until finally I felt *myself* spinning in a dark spiral and knew it was time to give up for the night.

Soon my whetted knife seemed to know what to do by itself—gouge and turn, gouge and turn, making slow but sure progress. In another couple of nights the scroll was finished. I smoothed off the rough edges with sandpaper and traced its spirals with proud but sore fingers. While it might not have looked like the ones in the Wish Book, it was better than nothing, and it was mine.

We were into the week before Christmas. Maman made us sugared pecans to eat after school.

Paulo was excited about what he'd get for Christmas. But I didn't have a prayer of getting what I really wanted, and I was busy doing something that I might get skinned alive for.

Then would come that time of the night when I went to work on my fiddle, and nothing else mattered.

My next task was to hollow out the center section of the neck just below the head, where the pegs would go in from the sides to hold the strings. It was sort of like hewing out a log to make a dugout canoe. It took some doing, too, to keep the walls thin enough to get the pegs through, yet thick enough to bear the stress.

I guess you'd say it was my pride that caused what happened next. When I should have been concentrating on the delicate job I was doing, my eyes strayed to admire my spiral fiddle head. That's when my knife slipped, stabbing into my left hand. I lost my balance and fell sideways off the bed, crashing into the night table and knocking the candle to the floor. Thankfully, its flame went out instead of setting something on fire. The washbasin on the table rattled but didn't fall.

"Félix?" Paulo mumbled in the dark.

"Hush," I whispered urgently. "Go back to sleep!" I was on all fours on the floor, with my hand to my mouth and the warm taste of blood on my tongue. The blade of the knife had jabbed into my hand just below my index finger, slicing through the hard callus that had built up there from all the levee shoveling. I felt around for the candle and the matches.

Just then Maman's voice called from downstairs, "Félix, what's going on up there?"

I jumped up and stumbled to the top of the stairs. "Nothing, Maman," I called. "I must've had a bad dream or something. I fell out of bed."

"Are you all right?" she said.

"Yes, ma'am, I just knocked the candle over."

"Well, goodnight, then."

I leaned against the wall until my heart stopped pounding, then made my way back to the table and lit the candle to survey the damage. Paulo sat up in his bed, staring at the telltale fiddle neck and knife sitting on my bed. He rubbed his eyes sleepily as I jumped to stand in front of the evidence.

"What's that on your bed?"

"Nothing."

"Whatcha doing sleeping with your pocketknife?" he said. My mouth opened, but no words would come out.

"I'm gonna go tell Maman." He stuck a skinny leg over the side of his bed.

"No!" I said, too loud. There was nothing I could do but let him in on my secret. "OK," I whispered, "but you have to promise not to tell."

"I don't have to promise nothin'. You better show me."

"I'm making myself a fiddle."

"A fiddle? How?"

"You'll see when it's done," I said, hoping to stall him.

"I'll tell. . . ."

"All right, all right," I said, and held up the neck and the cigar box. "I'm whittling the pieces with my knife. Then I'll put them all together and play it like 'Nonc Adolphe."

"I thought you were making something for me," he pouted.

"I will, as soon as I get done with this."

"You're gonna get in trouble," said Paulo. He yawned and got up to use the chamber pot. By the time he came back, he'd thought of his bribe. "I won't tell if you let me be in your band."

A nervous laugh jumped out of my mouth. "What band?"

"That's what you do when you play the fiddle—you

have a guitar, and an accordion, and a *'ti fer*. That's what I'm gonna play, the triangle. Can I?"

I shrugged. "Sure, Paulo, you can play the triangle in my band." The possibility of me ever playing the fiddle, much less having a band, seemed so far off I had to grin.

"Swear?"

"Sure, I swear," I said, spitting on my hand and crossing my heart.

He snuggled under the covers and fell asleep with a smug smile. Knowing Maman was awake downstairs, I blew out the candle and lay in the dark, the cut on my palm pulsing a warning.

Maman fussed over my hand the next day, rubbing on some of her plantain salve and wrapping it in a bandage. I told her I'd left my knife open by mistake and fallen on it in the dark, which technically wasn't a lie. But it left a guilty taste in my mouth, all the same.

There was one advantage to Paulo knowing about my fiddle—I didn't have to wait for him to go to sleep every night before I could start working. In fact, he was always trying to hurry me up so he could "join the band." He even announced at dinner that he wanted a *'ti fer* for Christmas, causing Maman to throw up her hands in exasperation.

By the time I blew out my candle on Christmas Eve, the fiddle neck was ready to go onto the cigar box. I sent up a prayer to the baby Jesus that He would understand what was making me go against my parents' wishes, that in my heart I didn't mean any harm.

But I couldn't tell whether He heard me or not.

On Christmas morning Papa told me to go look beside the fireplace. There stood a single-barrel shotgun.

"Go on, it's for you," said Papa. "It's 'Nonc Louis's old Remington—he was buying himself a new one. It might not look like much, but it's as true as the gospels." I picked it up, its well-worn stock warm in my hands, its barrel cold as a frog's belly. It was a long way from the Chicago Long-Range Wonder Hammerless Double-Barrel Breech-Loading Shotgun that I'd been wanting, but still it was a gun.

Paulo got a homemade set of toys that Papa had whittled for him, with dowels and wooden thread spools that he could fit into angles. Papa helped him build a windmill that turned when he blew on it, and Paulo was practically walking on the ceiling.

Paulo had made me a little set of men out of glued-together acorns. Feeling bad that I hadn't made him anything, I tickled him till he got the hiccups to let him know I liked them.

We pulled into the churchyard to find a crowd gathered off to one side. I jumped down and ran to see what the attraction was. There, like a giant Christmas bonbon, sat a bright red Chevrolet automobile.

"How do you like my mama's Christmas present?" crowed Chance. I should've known it was his.

I gaped at the sheer beauty of the thing. It had caramel-colored leather seats, black trim on its fenders, and a rumble seat in the back for extra passengers.

"I even got to drive it down the road a ways," said Chance, prancing around like a bantam rooster. "*And*—here's the best part"—he turned a handle and pulled open the trunk in the back—"look what *I* got for Christmas."

There sat a brand-new black and red Hohner accordion.

"Papa says nobody in our family's ever been able to play a lick of music," said Chance, "and he wants me to be the first. I'm thinking, if I can play something by Mardi Gras, I might ride on the musicians' wagon with your 'Nonc Adolphe!"

"And I'm going to play the *'ti fer*," said Paulo, appearing from nowhere. I waved him away.

"What'd you get for Christmas?" asked Chance.

The image of Chance riding the countryside at Mardi Gras with real musicians—with 'Nonc Adolphe—playing his shiny new accordion while I sat at home trying to squeak some sounds out of a cigar box, made me sick to my stomach. "A shotgun," I mumbled.

"Hey, that's great," said Chance. "I'm going to ask Papa if we can give you a ride in the Chevrolet after Mass."

I shrugged, feeling as if the air had been punched out of me.

When I went down on my knees during Mass, I prayed for the strength to conquer the envy that had settled over my heart. But I couldn't tell if that prayer got through, either.

That day I had my first ride in an automobile, a magical carriage out of some fairy tale that ran without horses and obeyed the will of human beings. Sure enough, it *was* like riding on a goose-down pillow. And I tried Chance's accordion, squeezing the buttons and pushing and pulling on the bellows until I found the notes of a scale.

"How'd you know how to do that?" asked Chance in awe. I shrugged.

That night I saw the pieces of my fiddle for what they were—some homemade scraps of wood and an old cigar box from the back of Monsieur Vidrine's store.

I put them away without touching them and dropped off into an anguished sleep.

Next morning Papa woke me before dawn to go hunt ducks with him, and within a couple of hours I'd bagged two pintails and a mallard. My gun's aim was as smooth and sure as spring rain, and Papa made a big fuss over my shooting. When we got back, wet and chilled to the bone, Maman set to making *roux* for a gumbo.

I'd wanted my own shotgun ever since I could remember. But now that I had it, I realized that it wasn't really a present for *me* as much as it was for the whole family. Now they expected me to bring home food for the supper table.

It felt as if every breath I took belonged to somebody besides me.

For the rest of the day we lazed around the kitchen, stretching our feet to the warmth of the stove, eating leftovers from the Christmas pork roast, and smelling the gumbo cooking. The sun set early, and after braving a bone-chilling drizzle for the evening chores, we ate and settled in front of the fire.

"Félix," said Papa, "will you read us some Bible verses?"

"Let's hear some Proverbs," said Maman.

Papa flipped to the well-worn Book of Proverbs and handed me the musty-smelling French Bible with its cracked leather cover. It had come down to Maman from her mother and her mother's mother.

I read Solomon's words almost from memory, without paying much attention, until I reached the part that read:

There are six things which the Lord hates, seven which are an abomination to him: haughty eyes, a lying tongue, and hands that shed innocent blood, a heart that devises wicked plans, feet that make haste to run to evil, a false witness who breathes out lies, and a man who sows discord among brothers.

I squirmed in my chair as I read on, about keeping your father's commandment and not forsaking your mother's teaching. My cheeks burned. When I got to the end, I closed the book, jumped up, and handed it to Papa, mumbling that I was tired. Tripping up the stairs, I sat on my bed and tried to drown out the sound of the words in my head.

I lay back and threw my arm over my face. It was too much, this being split down the middle. I wasn't an evil person, I wasn't. If I was Chance Guidry, I could build my fiddle right out in the open, with my mother patting my shoulder and saying how clever I was and my father laughing his big laugh. Of course, if I was Chance Guidry, all I'd have to do was ask for a fiddle, and it would appear like magic.

But I wasn't Chance, and I would never have a store-bought fiddle, and there was no telling what Maman and Papa would do if they found out what I was doing.

Reaching under my mattress, I pulled out the fiddle neck and held it onto the cigar box. It slipped into place with a satisfying neatness.

Once I attached it and cut a flat fingerboard to cover it, all I would have left to make was a handful of small pieces—the pegs, the bridge, and a leather tailpiece to hold the strings. Except for the bow, I figured I wasn't but a few days away from finishing.

It really did *look* like a fiddle. The workmanship was something to be proud of. But there was no knowing how it would sound until I'd made all the pieces and strung it up.

I knew deep down that I'd come too far to turn back now. Let my parents find out and do what they may, let Chance have his slick factory accordion. These pieces of wood and the possibility that lay silent in them were the only things that truly belonged to me.

I would finish my fiddle. And I would play it on the musicians' wagon at Mardi Gras, alongside of Chance and 'Nonc Adolphe.

chapter seven

A New Year

From then on I worked feverishly every night, pushing all doubt from my mind as I smuggled whatever tools and supplies I needed to my room. During the day Papa still had me working every spare moment, when the winter rains allowed, on building up the levee. We'd made a lot of progress but still had a long way to go.

Turning the open wooden cigar box upside down, I held the fiddle neck in place and nailed it on through the side wall. Now I had to make the fingerboard, which would fit on top of the neck and extend over the body of the fiddle. This was the part that 'Nonc's fingers were always dancing around on.

The advertisements in the Sears and Roebuck bragged about the fingerboards being made out of a black wood called ebony, so I figured I needed a hardwood. I found a dead branch from the pecan tree by the barn and sawed it into a thin slab at Papa's workbench. Then I spent several nights honing and sanding it into a slightly arched plank about the length of a ruler. This I glued on top of the neck.

Next came four pegs carved out of cypress, each one shaped like a small oar with a long handle. A skinny nail made a hole in each one to pass the strings through.

After that I had to whittle out two holes in each side of the head for the pegs to fit in. This was a delicate operation. The holes had to be alternately spaced and made to fit the tapering pegs. But I soon had them finished. Paulo was so excited he watched my every move from his bed, and I had to keep shushing him so he wouldn't attract Maman's attention. Eventually his eyelids would droop, and he'd fall asleep in spite of himself.

My last job on the body of the fiddle was to carve an F-shaped opening into each side of the top. I didn't know why they were there, maybe to let out the sound. *F for Félix, F for fiddle,* I thought as I set to work with the small blade of my knife.

Next I cut out a bridge from a small chunk of wood about an inch high and tapered down at the bottom, like a pyramid. Then I cut four little notches in its top, one for each string. This would hold the strings apart and up off the body of the fiddle.

The big question now was what to do for strings.

I wished I could waltz into Ardoin's Emporium and fiddle a tune until folks started tossing me money. But since that wasn't likely, I pulled my money jar out of the armoire. Four lonesome copper pennies glinted coldly in the candlelight. I didn't have a moth's chance in candlelight of coming up with enough money to buy strings. What I needed was some kind of wire, something much thinner than the baling wire we had in the barn. And some money to buy it with.

My only hope was *le petit bonhomme janvier,* the mysterious visitor who snuck in while Cajun children slept on New Year's Eve to leave something in their shoes.

Paulo shook me awake on January 1, 1915. "He came, he came!" he said excitedly. Sure enough, when I stuck my hand into my shoes, out came a shiny new dime.

"Merci, bon Dieu," I whispered. "Thank the good Lord."

School was out for another few days, and I knew I had to do something. So the next day, I took the biggest chance of my life.

I was supposed to be working on the levee while Papa tended to some business with 'Nonc Adolphe. But after I'd thrown a few shovelfuls of dirt, I struck out for town. It was the only way.

I sprinted the two miles, hoping not to meet anyone I knew on the road. My hands freezing and my stomach churning, I opened the door to Monsieur Vidrine's store. He was playing checkers with another customer by the wood stove. He heaved himself up and took his usual place behind the counter, rubbing his hands together. "My old arthritis kicks up in this weather, Félix," he said. "Everybody had a good Christmas at your house?"

"Yes, sir," I answered. But I was in no mood for small talk, and got right to the point. "Monsieur Vidrine," I whispered, "remember when you told me about your friend who made a fiddle?" He nodded. "Well, I gotta know what he used for strings."

He leaned toward me.

"He used some wire," he said. "But I recall he always had trouble with that." His eyes gleamed conspiratorially. "Now, if it was me, you know what I'd try? Screen wire. It's fine enough to do the job, it seems to me."

There it was again, the Vidrine glimmer of hope.

"Your daddy still hasn't put screens on your windows, has he?" he asked.

I shook my head. "Could I buy some off of you?"

Monsieur Vidrine rubbed his chin. "You better come on in the back with me."

I followed him into the stockroom, which was piled to the ceiling with crates and boxes and sacks, and smelled of lamp oil and old potatoes and axle grease. It was so cold we breathed out little white clouds as we made our way to the carpentry supplies. Monsieur Vidrine reached up to a high shelf and pulled down a roll of screening.

"This stuff is worth its weight in gold in the summertime, Félix," he said, "but nobody buys any in this kind of weather." He took a pair of heavy shears and cut off a narrow length. "Now, let's get back inside 'fore we freeze our toes off."

My heart thumped as he coiled the tiny length of screening. "And I need a spool of white thread."

"For your bow?"

I nodded. "If I have enough money, that is. All I've got is fourteen cents."

Monsieur Vidrine looked over his tiny gold-rimmed glasses. "You better take two spools of thread," he said. "Let's see, with the discount for my good customers, that'll be—" he scribbled figures on a pad "—about fourteen cents."

I grinned with relief and handed over my sweaty coins.

"Still just between you and me?" he asked.

"Yes, sir, if you don't mind."

He pretended to turn a key on his lips. I sprinted back across the prairie toward home, thankful that at least *one* person was on my side. That afternoon I worked at double speed on the levee, trying to make up for my misdeed and to ease my conscience.

I would have gotten away with it, except that Paulo saw me leave.

He didn't tell on me, I'll give him that much. But he was waiting to pounce on me when I got back, with a mouthful of questions I didn't want to answer. So he'd had plenty of time to think up a good bribe.

"I want your pocketknife," he pronounced triumphantly.

"Not on your life!" I cried.

"Then I'm telling," he said with a nod of his head for emphasis. And I knew he would, too.

"But I need it to finish my fiddle," I pleaded.

"I already thought of that. I'll give it to you at night, and you give it back to me in the morning."

I had no choice. I reached into my pocket and pulled out my prize possession. Paulo snatched it with his grubby little hand.

Then he went right out and nearly cut off his thumb with it the very next day, and told Maman I'd given it to him. That earned me a long lecture about how irresponsible I was and how I was supposed to look out for my little brother instead of endangering his life.

And then they took away my knife.

My pocket felt empty without its weight. It was as if I'd lost my best friend. I turned a deaf ear and a stony face to Paulo's fervent pleas for forgiveness. The only consolation was that I had already finished most of the carving for my fiddle. I only had one more piece to make: the tailpiece to hold the strings on at the base of the fiddle.

Struggling with a butcher knife on Papa's workbench, I managed to cut a scrap of cowhide into a fan shape. Then I poked four holes, one for each string, into the wide end of the leather tailpiece.

But how would I attach it to the lower side of the fiddle? The pictures in the Sears and Roebuck showed a knob that the tailpiece slipped over. I ended up sneaking downstairs in the dark to pilfer Maman's kitchen knife, which I used to carve and insert a little wooden plug at the chin end of the fiddle. After poking two holes in the narrow end of the tailpiece, I ran a strip of cowhide through them, which I slipped over the plug.

Now I had the body of the fiddle, complete with its carved neck, and a little pile of pieces that went on it. I got out the wad of screening. The wires were woven over and under, just like the cloth Maman wove on her loom. Unraveling four long wires, I thought about how the strings were sort of like the fiddle's vocal cords. Without them there would be no music.

On a violin, each string was supposed to be a little thicker than the next, but I had to give up on that idea and hope for the best. I threaded each length through one of the four holes in the leather tailpiece, twisting them around to hold them on. Then I pulled them up toward the head and, following the Sears pictures, threaded each one into the nailhole in the four pegs. Starting on the right-hand side, I tightened each peg until the wire was nearly taut, two on the left and two on the right.

Next I slipped the wooden bridge under the strings in the center of the fiddle's body, between the two F-shaped holes. That way the strings were held apart and up off the body of the fiddle.

My fingers trembled as I began the last task—tuning

the strings to their four different pitches. The Wish Book had an advertisement for "Violin Tuning Pipes" tuned to *sol, re, la,* and *mi.* I had a good idea of what that sounded like from music lessons at school.

Starting on the left side, I twisted the peg until the wire held enough tension to give off a low *thud.* I kept turning until it was more like a *plunk.* Then I moved on to the next one. Each one was harder than the last because the wire had to be pulled tighter each time.

Finally, I was done. It was time to see if my fiddle had a voice.

My heart swelled as my chin clamped down on the end of the cigar box. Holding the fiddle up with my left hand, I tucked my elbow under like 'Nonc Adolphe and pressed down on the wires. Then I reached up with the index finger of my right hand and plucked the top string. *Dink,* it said daintily. *Donk,* said the next one. *Dank,* said the third string, and *doink,* said the lowest one.

A giddiness came over me, a lightheaded joy that I'd never felt before. There was the possibility of music in this cigar box, a possibility that hadn't been there before I put it in with my own two hands.

Pride filled me like warm spring sunshine. Thinking back to the last New Year's, I couldn't even remember what I'd done or what had mattered to me then. Everything before the night of the party at Chance's house, when I'd heard 'Nonc Adolphe play, seemed pale and far away. And this year was starting out to be the best ever.

I had made myself a fiddle.

But that was before I heard the *crunch* and before I watched the fiddle bend itself in half right there in my hands. The end of the cigar box where the neck was attached had crumpled under the tension of the strings, leaving the pieces dangling from the wires.

I crawled into my bed in despair, hot tears rolling down my cheeks. Maybe God was punishing me for doing what I was doing. Maybe it would never work, and I would never be a fiddler. For the first time since I was a little kid, I cried myself to sleep.

"When you've got a problem," Papa always said, "sleep on it. It'll always look different in the morning."

As usual, he was right. When I looked closely at my broken fiddle in the morning light, it didn't look so bad. The lightweight wood of the cigar box just needed re-inforcing.

It would've been a whole lot easier if I'd had my knife. But if something means enough to you, you'll do anything to make it work.

After my usual stint on the levee the next day, Papa set me to sharpening the shovels at his workbench. That gave me time to saw a small rectangle out of a cypress shingle.

That night I nailed it inside the cigar box to brace the broken side.

Once again I turned the pegs, cringing as I tightened the E-string to its high pitch. But this time it held. I danced a cautious little jig.

Now all I needed was a bow.

For this, I "borrowed" a crosscut saw and hightailed it out to the hickory tree back of the barn near the coulee. I shinnied up the trunk and cut a branch the right size for a bow, about as big around as my finger. As I'd hoped, it bent itself easily in the right curve.

Ducking into the barn, I sprinted up the ladder to sit on my throne. Working quickly, I sawed a notch in either end of the hickory switch, then tried bending the switch between my knees into a curve. It kept popping out, so I stuffed it into a wooden crate, which held it in a wide curve. Then I set to wrapping the thread from one end to the other and back again, over and over, fitting the thread into a notch each time. When I ran out of thread, I tied it off and, holding my breath, pried the stick out of the crate.

The shape held.

Stuffing one end of the bow down my pants leg and pulling my shirt over the other, I limped like Long John Silver across the yard and up the stairs to my room.

Pulling out the bow, I retrieved my fiddle from under

the bed. My breath caught when I looked at my handiwork in the light of day. Grasping it in a fiddler's hold with my left hand, I set the bow down on the strings with my right and pulled it across. *Scri-i-itch*. Not exactly a golden note. I retuned the string and tried again. This time it was more of a high *z-z-z-z*, like a mosquito in your ear. Better. The next time it made a sound that I was sure was a musical note. Maybe not an A, but it was definitely music.

I had a bow. I had a fiddle. And I had a fever burning inside of me that heated up with every note I played.

"La Chanson de Mardi Gras"

I decided that my first song would be *"La Chanson de Mardi Gras,"* the sad-sounding melody that was played over and over at Mardi Gras. Mardi Gras means "Fat Tuesday," a last day of revelry and meat-eating before the strict forty days of Lent leading up to Easter. Every year, costumed men rode horses around the countryside, playing tricks and acting crazy and begging for chickens and rice to go into a big gumbo that night. If I could learn that song, I'd be ready to play with Chance on the musicians' wagon, which followed the riders around on their yearly quest.

Since everyone wore costumes on Mardi Gras, I figured maybe I could disguise myself, and no one would ever know it was me. If I could pull it off, I wouldn't care what happened after that.

But first I had to learn to play.

An entire warm Sunday afternoon stretched in front

of me, with no shovels and no levee in sight. Out in the barn loft I leaned back on my hay throne and tucked the fiddle under my chin. When I held it in my hands, it didn't matter a fig what anybody else was doing. I was in heaven.

Remembering how 'Nonc Adolphe looked when he played, I swung the bow up to the strings with a flourish and pulled it across the strings, just like he'd shown me.

I pressed a finger onto the first string. *Proing!* The tension sprang and the screen wire sagged.

Setting down the bow, I grasped the peg and turned till the string was taut again. But when I set the bow to it, it sprang again. This time I ignored it and played softly on the other three strings, though they were already out of tune themselves.

Finally, I had to cut two more pegs with thicker stems, so thick I had to jam them into the holes. After that they held, and the top string made something like a high *mi* sound.

But no matter how tight the wires stayed, I couldn't get much more than a low buzz out of the fiddle. To make matters worse, the sewing thread kept wearing through and dangling off the bow.

That night, poring over the pictures in the Sears and Roebuck, I hit upon the solution to one of my problems. It mentioned a bow made with "the finest horsehair." That had to mean from the horse's tail.

As soon as I got the chance the next day, I put old Henri to good use. Cooing softly to him in case he got any ideas of kicking me, I grabbed a hank of his tail hair. He swung his head around and glared at me as I hacked at it with Maman's sewing scissors. I promised him it would grow back, and he went back to swishing imaginary flies.

Once I'd washed the hair and strung it onto my hickory stick, my bow worked much better.

But my fiddle still didn't sound anywhere close to the music in my head.

School started up again after the long winter break, and Mademoiselle Sonnier cracked the whip on us harder than ever. I would try to concentrate on the words she wrote on the blackboard, but they kept dissolving into an image of my fiddle before my eyes. No matter how I tried to chase it away, it haunted me from the moment I woke up to the moment I closed my eyes at night.

At lunchtime Chance came up to me with a big grin. "How come you've been so scarce lately, Félix?" he asked. "Whatcha been doin'?"

"Nothin'" was all I could answer. By then I'd grown used to carrying around the secret of my fiddle inside of me, like a gold nugget tucked inside a hidden pouch. I was afraid if I exposed it to the light of day, and to Chance's judgment, it might turn out to be nothing more than fool's gold.

Besides, I didn't really want to hear any more about his accordion and his Chevrolet. Finally, he shrugged and went off to join the other boys.

It was my turn to stay after school to clean the blackboards and the erasers and sweep the floor. Forlornly, I watched Chance and Paulo and all the others file out into the afternoon sunshine. But when I emerged half an hour later, covered with chalk dust and aggravation, Chance appeared around the corner of the schoolhouse.

"It took you long enough," he said. "What'd you do, lick the blackboard clean? Come on, I'll buy you a *pop rouge*."

I squinted into the pale sun. "I don't need your charity," I heard myself say. Something seemed to burst inside of me, and more words came rushing out. "You think you're so great, with your Chevrolet automobile and your horse and your *pop rouge* and your store-bought accordion that I bet you can't even play. I'm sick to death of you showing off, just because your daddy's rich."

First a puzzled look crossed Chance's face, then his face flushed an angry red. "Sorry I asked," he said. He spun around and stalked off, leaving me with a sick feeling in my stomach.

I wanted to call out after him, but nothing would come out of my mouth. Now I had lost my best friend.

The Sears and Roebuck catalogue talked about different varnishes on different instruments, and I got to thinking how maybe that would help my fiddle sound better. So I gave it two good coats of the Japalac that Papa kept in the toolshed. That gave it a shine like a new penny. But the sounds that came out still sounded like a crosscut saw instead of the clear, plaintive sounds I was after. And the wires were driving me crazy.

One afternoon I found myself with a few spare minutes before chore time, so I tucked my fiddle under my coat and sprinted the half-mile to the woods along the back edge of the cornfield. It was chilly and damp under the ancient trees, and strangely quiet. When I was younger, they used to say it was where Madame Grands-Doigts lived, a wicked old witch with gnarled and twisty fingers. If you weren't good, she'd sneak into your room at night and pull your toes.

Of course, none of those stories scared me anymore, but I still looked over my shoulder every now and then out of habit. Climbing the fat trunk of a huge live oak, I found a comfortable seat in the crook of a limb. There I let loose and played as loud as my homemade fiddle would play, even lowering it every once in a while to sing a verse at the top of my voice. It felt good, like I was being let out of a box.

As I was sawing away on my perch, I heard a rustling down below, from back the way I'd come. I stopped playing and listened. It was getting closer. Was it a deer? A fox? I held my breath as whatever it was came into view.

It was a beast, all right—one named Paulo. The little runt had followed me.

He was getting too cocky, and it was time to teach him a lesson. Pulling my legs up into the tree, I began to make moaning noises, first low, then working up to high and shrill. Paulo stopped dead in his tracks, his eyes bulging out of his head and his face turning white as a cotton boll. He stood there frozen for a second, then turned tail and bolted for home. I laughed so hard I nearly fell out of the tree.

That night I waited till he was almost asleep before I sneaked out of bed and, cackling like Madame Grands-Doigts, pulled his toes with my cold fingers. He screamed bloody murder.

"It's Madame Grands-Doigts," I cackled, "and I like to eat little boys who follow their brothers into the woods." I kept cackling as I got back into bed.

"Just you wait, Félix," Paulo said, low and breathless. "I'll get you for that."

The January days crawled by. Chance no longer waited for me at recess and at lunch but went off with a group of other boys without so much as a glance my way. If I hadn't had my fiddle to keep me company, I might have shriveled up and died from lonesomeness.

'Nonc Adolphe had been pretty scarce, so Maman and

Papa decided we would stop by his house on the way back from our monthly trip to Eunice.

We headed for town in a cold Saturday drizzle. The mud sucked at the wagon wheels and at the horses' hooves as I hunkered down under an old quilt.

Eunice bustled with activity even in the rain that choked the smoke back down the chimneys. As we passed the imposing front of Ardoin's Emporium, I thought longingly of all those little packets of fiddle strings guarded by Amos Voorhies in that case upstairs. There were no such treasures in the general mercantile up the street where we did our trading.

Papa ticked off his list to the clerk behind the counter, and Maman fingered fabrics and tallied prices. When the wagon was finally loaded, Papa surprised us with a stop at the ice cream shop. The cold sugary taste of vanilla made me smile, something I hadn't done much of lately.

We ate our lunch of boiled eggs and fried rice cakes on the way to 'Nonc Adolphe's. As we pulled up under the big trees in the front yard, the unmistakable whine of a fiddle drifted out into the gray afternoon. The sound cut a nick in my heart like my pocketknife had done to my hand.

'Nonc was mighty surprised to see us. He stumbled around, picking up rags and paintbrushes and pulling paper off the furniture so we could sit down, all the while apologizing for the mess. But the truth was, it looked a whole lot better than the last time I'd seen it. The parlor sported a fresh coat of plaster, the broken windows had been repaired, and the dust that covered everything was from hard work instead of neglect. Even Maman complimented him on the job.

'Nonc made coffee for Papa and Maman, and Paulo and I drank root beer. 'Nonc sat nervously a minute, then jumped to his feet, saying, "Marie, let me show you something I found when I was cleaning out the attic." He disappeared into the other room and came out with a paper parcel tied up in string. "This belongs to you, if I recall."

"What is it?" said Paulo.

Maman struggled with the string until she finally got it untied. When the paper fell open, her hand flew to her mouth and she uttered a little "Oh!"

Papa's smile stretched from one ear to the other. "Would you look at that?" he said.

"What is it?" Paulo whined insistently. I was glad he said it so I didn't have to.

"This, boys," said Papa, "is a Parisian Gainsborough hat. It was once the height of fashion. Your mama was wearing it the night I met her."

Out of the paper came an old black velvet hat all piled up with black ribbons and red roses, with a big red feather sticking up from the side. Paulo and I giggled. It was hard to imagine Maman, who never wore anything but her sturdy homemade sunbonnet or her straw hat, going out in public with that on her head. Her face had softened, and she ran her hands over the velvet as if she was petting a colt's nose.

"This hat caused me so much grief," said Maman. "You see, I saved up my money and bought it against my parents' wishes. And then I'd wear it whenever I thought I could get away with it."

"And you got caught?" asked Paulo.

She nodded. "My grandmama chaperoned me to a dance and saw me wearing it. Papa never let me forget it."

"I fell in love with your mother the minute I saw her in it," said Papa. "And so did every other boy in the parish. But your grandpapa was so mad at her, he didn't let her go to a *bal* for a long time after that, so I had to wait a long time to do my courting." He kissed Maman's cheek.

She sighed. "I remember thinking I'd die if I didn't have this hat," she said.

I couldn't believe my ears. So Maman had once wanted something bad enough to go against her parents, too.

"But it wasn't worth what happened afterward."

"Aw, but I remember that smile, that twinkle in your eyes," said 'Nonc Adolphe. "Where did they go?"

Maman sighed again. "Things were simpler in those days, Adolphe," she said, setting her mouth back in its straight line. "Before I had to bury my babies out back, before life was such a struggle."

"That's why you've got to grab onto joy whenever you get the chance," said 'Nonc Adolphe, leaning forward and clenching his fist like joy was floating in the air in front of him.

The room fell silent except for the dripping of rain off the roof. Then Papa stood up and held out his hand to Maman. "Would you play us a tune, Adolphe?" he said. "'La Valse du Bayou,' that waltz Marie used to like so much."

"Mais oui," said 'Nonc, jumping up and grabbing his fiddle. And before Maman could protest, Papa had pulled her to her feet and grabbed her around the waist. At first she stepped woodenly to the slow, sad song, but finally she let herself be led in wide, graceful circles around the room. Her skirt swung out behind her, and she looked up into Papa's eyes till the song was over.

Maman glanced at us and seemed to come back to her senses. "We'd best get home," she said. "There's work to be done." She tried to hand the hat back to 'Nonc Adolphe, but he shook his head.

"Keep it, Marie," he said, "to remind you to smile."

She ducked her head and went out the door. The rest of us followed. I was admiring the repair job 'Nonc had done on the front gallery steps when my eyes fell on something in the mud nearby.

Was it a fiddle string? In a flash I recalled that day I'd gone to town with 'Nonc, when he'd put on the new set of strings we'd bought at Ardoin's. He'd thrown the old ones off the porch!

Hanging back as 'Nonc followed the rest of them to the wagon, I jumped down and pulled at the end of the string. As it coiled itself out of the mud, it pulled two more along with it, and I felt around till I found the fourth one. Stuffing them into my coat pocket, I jumped into my place in the wagon. It seemed to be a day for smiles.

After I cleaned them up and put them on, the new strings worked like a charm. At last my fiddle would stay in tune, and I could get a new, richer tone out of it that came closer to what I heard in my head.

The horsehair of the bow still skittered across the surface of the strings, proving the need for rosin, which I figured was nothing more than pine sap. Knowing how a pine bark beetle will drill a hole in the skin of a tree, I found a fat old white pine in the forest, and bored a small hole down into the sapwood. All I needed after that was patience for the sap to rise and drip out in the spring.

Meanwhile, I got down to serious business. My fiddle now lived up in the barn loft, tucked inside a flour sack and under a pile of hay. I hid myself out there whenever I could, cold or no cold, levee or no levee. For a while I just sawed back and forth on the open strings, trying to get a fuller sound from each pull of the bow. Then I began setting down one finger at a time. As I got braver, I'd put down a second finger, and a third. I started on the lowest string, the G, and hunted around for every note up the scale. The notes slowly began to fall in line, and my fingers soon learned where to plunk themselves down to play in tune.

Mind you, it wasn't anywhere near as easy as 'Nonc made it look. First you had to get the string in tune, then you had to get your finger in the right place, then you had to pull the bow across with enough pressure to make a clear note. It was a bugger of a job.

There were times when I nearly gave up, it was so hard. But I couldn't, so I kept on trying. A hard callus began to form on the tip of each finger of my left hand from all the pressing down on the strings. And before long I was making a little music.

I'll admit, I was completely obsessed with it. All I thought about, no matter what else I was doing, was finding time to get back to my fiddle.

Luckily, it was a rainy winter, so there wasn't much to do on the levee. After school when the weather was bad, I'd make a beeline for the barn and sometimes, if Papa didn't need me, I'd stay there and play all afternoon. Other times, even though the weather was still cold, I'd hightail it out to the woods and climb up into that notch in the oak tree and play for the squirrels. Or carry it along with my shotgun on hunting expeditions, celebrating a kill with a song.

Once I got good at playing notes, I started trying to lay down the tune of *"La Chanson de Mardi Gras."* The notes skipped around over different strings, and it took me days of frustrating practice to learn the barest bones of it. But at last I began to figure out the pattern to the melody, and it got so my fingers would find their place before my brain got there. After playing it about a thousand times, I could get through it from beginning to end without any mistakes.

That first song was the hardest one. After that I sort of got the hang of it. There were certain patterns that showed up in different songs, and once you learned the pattern in one, you could use it in another. A reel and a contredanse were what I learned next. I discovered that all those songs I'd been hearing all my life were rolling around in my head, and it got easier and easier to get them out on those four strings.

I was feeling pretty full of myself. I even got so I'd hear a new tune in my head, one that was all mine and nobody else's, and then I'd make it come out of the fiddle. I named the first one I made up "Vidrine's Reel," for all the help Monsieur Vidrine had given me.

The more I practiced, the more it seemed that playing

my fiddle could make the world disappear. Sometimes I was no longer sitting in the barn or in the tree, I was somewhere far away, traveling on the melody coming out beneath my fingers. There was no worry about Maman or guilt about Chance, no limits to how far I could spin myself out.

It was better than a ticket on a southbound train.

Meanwhile, Mardi Gras neared. Some days that thought filled me with dread. Other times I didn't know if I could stand the wait. I got used to living with butterflies flapping around in my stomach.

It was time to figure out a good disguise.

Mardi Gras Madness

When I was little, the events of Mardi Gras Day both terrified and fascinated me. Papa always stayed home from the fields that day, and we all waited expectantly for the craziness that we knew would arrive sooner or later. At last Papa would shade his eyes into the distance and say, "Here they come."

First you'd hear a faint commotion coming from down the road, like the angry buzzing of bees. Then you'd see a clump of fifteen or twenty men on horseback coming toward you, dressed in ragtag costumes of yellow and red and purple and green, with masks on their faces and tall pointed hats like dunces or queens, or flat hats like scholars. As they drew closer and finally stopped outside the fence, you could hear them singing the Mardi Gras song over and over.

Dressing up in a beggar-like costume was a way to be somebody besides yourself and go kind of crazy on that last day before Lent. I knew my costume had to be the best disguise ever so nobody, and I mean nobody, would know who I was.

I found an old pair of Papa's overalls in the ragbag, along with some colorful fabric scraps. Burning the midnight oil again, but being extra careful not to wake Paulo, I worked needle and thread in awkward stitches, trying to sew on rows of tattered-looking fringe. Finally, I had most of the denim fabric covered with fringe, and then made a tall pointed hat, or *capuchon,* out of heavy paper.

The most important part would be my mask. I decided on the old way of molding wet cheesecloth soaked in starch to my face.

I had to make a wild guess as to how much of Maman's starch to add to a bucket half-filled with water, which I had carried up to the barn loft. It turned out I might've put in a bit too much, since the finished mask would've stood up to a baseball bat. After soaking a length of gauzy cheesecloth that I'd folded to the right size in the soupy mixture, I squeezed out the excess liquid. Then, lying down on the loft floor, I laid the cold, wet cheesecloth on my face and mashed it into my eyes, around my nose, and under my chin.

Lying there still as death, I felt my heart jump at every rustle and creak I heard, for fear someone would find me. At last, after an hour or so, the starch began to set up. I lifted the sticky fabric off my face and shaped it over a face-sized mound of hay to finish drying.

The next day I trimmed the edges, cut out eyes and a breathing hole, and attached lengths of string to tie it on the back of my head. Using a lead pencil, I drew on eyes, eyebrows, a mouth, and even a thin mustache like 'Nonc Adolphe's. When I fit it onto my face, even my own mother wouldn't have recognized me.

The night before Mardi Gras, Papa announced that we would spend the day working on the levee.

"But, Papa, it's Mardi Gras," I said, hearing the desperation in my own voice. "You never work on Mardi Gras."

"That levee doesn't know what day it is," said Papa. "We're too close to finishing it to stop now. Planting time will be here before we know it."

As I lay in my bed that night, I didn't even have to make a decision. I'd waited too long and worked too hard to miss the Mardi Gras ride and let Chance do it without me. I would sneak out and take the consequences later.

I didn't actually wake up on Mardi Gras morning, because I'd never really gotten to sleep. Before the break of day I swung my feet to the floor, dressed, and sneaked down the stairs and out into the cold foggy day. I milked Caillette, fed the sleepy chickens, and slopped the hogs before taking off on foot across the prairie toward town. A satchel carrying my costume and my fiddle bounced on my back as I made my way through the cold drizzle.

When I got to the edge of L'Anse Rougeau, I ducked behind a shed to pull on my costume. I could see the colorful riders gathered in front of Monsieur Vidrine's store. Against the gray morning they looked like a wacky flock of parrots in their ragbag and gunnysack costumes. Off to the side a farm wagon harnessed to two sturdy horses was loaded with chicken cages up front, and hay bales lining the back for the musicians to sit on.

There lay my destiny. I hid in the shadows, suddenly too terrified to move. But out of the murmur of voices came a cracked laugh that could only have come from Chance. I pulled my mask over my face.

Monsieur Vidrine rode by in his purple captain's cape, carrying a white flag on a stick. More than anything at that moment I wished I could call out to him for courage. But just then he waved the flag and shouted, "All right, boys, let's fall in. The *courir's* about to roll."

A whoop went up from the horseback riders, and several costumed musicians climbed up into the bed of the wagon and sat on the hay bales. One of them, dressed in a bright green costume and holding a brand-new shiny black accordion, took a seat toward the back of the wagon bed.

Peeking around the corner of the store, I watched the riders fall into a rowdy column in front of the wagon. My mouth went dry, my heart thumped in my chest, and my lungs suddenly couldn't find enough air. The wagon wheels began to turn, slowly at first, then picking up speed and moving away. Paralyzed by panic, I could do nothing but watch.

Then, as if something had pushed me from behind, I found myself running toward the wagon. Slinging my gunnysacked fiddle ahead of me, I climbed up and collapsed into the wagon bed.

There was Chance in his green costume, a screen mask with a carrot-shaped nose covering his face. To his right was a fiddler I was pretty sure was Moïse Thibodeaux, a guitar player I didn't recognize, a couple of triangle players, one of which had to be old Jean Boutté, and Monsieur Joseph Hébert, whom I knew from his well-worn accordion. I felt like I was stepping into another life, into the skin of someone who wasn't me and wouldn't be until the clock struck midnight.

"Qui c'est ça?" said Monsieur Hébert. "Who's that?"

I'd left my voice somewhere back there on the prairie, so I just shrugged.

"Mystery musician, eh?" said Monsieur Hébert. "Well, we'll see if you're any good."

Ahead, the Mardi Gras riders had fallen into a rough and rowdy column as the procession led its slow pace down the road. "Come on, boys, let's hit it!" said Monsieur Hébert, and he bellowed out the first notes of the Mardi Gras song.

Just then a rider galloped up behind us, shouting, "Hold on, there, you ain't leaving without me!" I recognized the roan horse, then 'Nonc Adolphe, dressed in a long black coat and a black scarf with eyeholes cut in it that made him look like a bandit. Handing up his fiddle, he swung a leg onto the moving wagon and tied Gypsy to the back. Grinning at the welcoming cries from the others, he pulled out his fiddle and joined in the song.

My stomach sat in my throat, my hands felt paralyzed. I was supposed to get out my fiddle, but I couldn't bring myself to do it.

As the musicians churned out the droning melody, 'Nonc closed his eyes and opened his mouth, and out came the words:

> *Les Mardi Gras, ça vient de tout partout*
> *Tout alentour, le tour du moyeu,*
> *Ça passe une fois par an pour demander la charité*
> *Quand même c'est une patate, une poule grasse ou des*
> *gratons.*

It was a song that was burned into our brains every year at this time, like carols at Christmas. It talked about the riders going all over the neighborhood once a year to ask for charity—a fat hen, a sweet potato, or some cracklings—anything that could be used for the big meal at the end of the day.

Capitaine, Capitaine, voyage ton flag,
Allons chez l'autre voisin
Demander la charité pour vous-autres,
Vous-autres, vous venez nous rejoindre
Oui, au gumbo ce soir.

"Captain, Captain, wave your flag, let's go to the next house, to ask for charity. Come join us at the gumbo tonight." As the song progressed, I watched as Chance pulled out his accordion. I didn't know where he found the courage, but shyness had never been Chance's problem. He joined right in and, even though it took him a minute to find the beat, pretty soon he was stumbling along. 'Nonc Adolphe looked at him and then at his accordion, and I was sure he recognized both. Then his eyes swung around to me, and I looked down at my feet, my cheeks burning despite the cold.

They played the song three or four times before 'Nonc played a flashy ending. Then he looked straight at me and said, "Musicians only on this wagon."

"That's right," said the guitar player. "Put up or get out."

Monsieur Hébert started up a fast one-step, a Mardi Gras drinking song about hitting the bottom of the bottle, and everyone joined in. I ordered my hands to open my sack and pull out my fiddle. All eyes were on me.

The little fiddle looked foolish in the light of day, but

I had no choice. Heavy as stone, my right elbow came up and the bow dropped to the strings. I scratched around for a hold on the tune they were playing.

After a while I found the key, and just played any notes that matched the tune. It was one of the worst moments of my life, and I had only myself to blame.

The song ended at last. "Well, looka here," said the triangle player next to me. "It's a little homemade fiddle—my daddy used to have him one of those. Go ahead on, man."

I ducked my head and stared at my knees until the next song started up. Thankfully, it was a waltz I knew, and it came out better than the last. My elbow loosened up, and my fingers began to find the right notes. After that one, they did *"La Chanson de Mardi Gras"* again, and this time I jumped in on all four strings. A few verses into the song, after 'Nonc had taken a solo, he pointed his bow at me. "Take a ride, fiddler," he said.

My heart stopped in my chest, and for a frozen second I couldn't breathe. But then my mind gave me a prod, reminding me of what I'd gone through to get on this wagon. I knew the song, and all I had to do was play it. So I closed my eyes and let the music take over.

The song came out of the tips of my fingers and out of the hairs on the bow and out of somewhere around the middle of my chest. My little fiddle did its best to throw its music out for all to hear. Suddenly, I felt my mouth open wide and the words jump out of my throat. I sang in a voice that was high and clear, and I sang them from the inside of the Mardi Gras.

When the verse ended, the accordion took over again, but I saw several heads nod in approval and heard a *"Bien bon"* from across the wagon. I smiled shakily under my mask. 'Nonc Adolphe stared at me for a long moment before pointing his bow at Chance to jump in on his accordion. Chance bumbled it midway through the song, though, and Monsieur Hébert had to take over for him.

As the song ended, I tucked my cold feet into the straw on the wagon bed and found that there were hot bricks buried there to keep our feet warm. Someone poked me in the ribs, and the *'ti fer* player on my right handed me a pint bottle of whiskey.

Maman had a strong opinion of liquor, and here it was being put into my hand. But a wild giddiness had replaced my fear. My fingers wrapped around the bottle, and I lifted my mask just high enough to take a swig, careful not to let anyone see my face.

It rasped at my throat going down, then burned a hole in my stomach where it landed. I had to struggle not to choke or cough. The man gestured for me to pass it on to the accordion player on my left, who never even hesitated before taking a long pull.

By then we'd pulled up at the Bergeron farm just outside of town. I saw flasks of whiskey going in and out of the horseback riders' pockets, too, as they waited impatiently outside the yard while Monsieur Vidrine rode up to the house.

"Voulez-vous recevoir les Mardi Gras?" he asked, meaning, "Will you receive the Mardi Gras riders?" Of course Monsieur Bergeron said yes, and the captain waved his flag.

Suddenly, the riders whipped their horses into a gallop and charged into the yard, whooping and hollering like wild banshees as we played the Mardi Gras song. They started doing tricks, standing up and balancing in their saddles, or turning headstands and cartwheels, or grabbing Madame Bergeron and her daughters and dancing a wild two-step. After they'd entertained the farm family for a good while, Monsieur Vidrine asked if they had anything to give for the Mardi Gras.

Old Monsieur Bergeron disappeared into the henhouse and came out with a red hen tucked under his arm. I saw his arm go up as the hen was launched into the air, coming down with her wings flapping wildly between the camellia bushes in the front yard.

Chaos followed as the riders jumped off their horses and took out after that chicken like it was the goose that laid the golden egg. She led them on a pretty good chase until one of them finally landed her with a flying tackle.

He held her up as a trophy, and Monsieur Vidrine brought her to the wagon, where she was put into one of the cages up front for the gumbo that night.

Another whiskey bottle was pressed into my hand, and this time the sweet firewater went down easier, warming me to my toes.

The gray day lightened a little as the sun climbed into the sky. But as the songs spun out and the whiskey went round, I ceased to care about the riders on their horses, or the families gathered in the yards to receive the Mardi Gras, or about anything but pulling note after note after note out of my fiddle. It was as if the world had shrunk to the size of the wagon bed and the men within its wooden sides, and nothing mattered but the sounds our souls were putting out.

After what might have been minutes or might have been hours, someone handed us a plate of hot *boudin,* and my stomach was grateful for the rice and meat to calm the lapping waves of whiskey. As I picked up my fiddle again, my head began to feel as if it was no longer connected to my neck. But with each swallow of liquor, the music I played seemed to get better and better.

Suddenly, my fingers slackened on my bow, and it flew into the fragrant hay. 'Nonc grinned under his bandit mask as he reached down and picked it up. "Take it easy on that stuff, fiddler, or you'll be sorry," he said, handing the bow back to me. I tried to say *merci,* but my tongue had swelled up in my mouth and didn't leave enough room for the word.

And that's how it happened that I didn't realize we'd gotten to my own house. We'd just started up on the Mardi Gras song again. Feeling a burst of confidence, I stood up on shaky legs to take my solo run. 'Nonc Adolphe hissed, "Sit down, fiddler," but I just figured he didn't want me stealing his spotlight. The notes dazzled out into the middle of the day, and I sang a verse. As I finished, a bottle of whiskey was put into my hand.

I raised my mask to fit the flask to my lips, no longer so careful to hide my face. When I tilted my head to let the golden liquid pour down my throat, the sky swung in slow circles above me.

Just then one of the drunken riders bumped into the lead horse, and the wagon lurched forward. I staggered a dizzy step sideways, toward the open back end of the wagon.

That's when I saw the faces staring at me from across the yard.

One was Maman's, frozen into a look of fury. Beside her stood Papa and Paulo.

Still reeling, I groped with my arm for something to hold onto. But there was nothing.

I lurched headlong into thin air.

The seconds stretched themselves out as I drifted slowly, slowly toward the ground. I saw Maman's mouth open to call my name. And then I closed my eyes and let it happen.

My shoulder struck the ground with a *thud* that sent a jolt through my whole body. My head hit and bounced up. As the rest of me came down, something in my shoulder gave way with a crunch.

My fiddle went flying across the road and into a ditch.

Breaks

I sank into some deep black place. The next thing I knew I was swirling back from far away, and someone was turning me over and pulling off my mask. I heard a scream and realized it came from me. A sharp pain sliced through my shoulder and down the side of my body. Then faces were hovering over me; one of them was Maman's, one was 'Nonc Adolphe's, and one was Chance's.

"That's his collarbone, *non?*" said 'Nonc Adolphe.

"Take it easy, son," said Papa's voice, "we'll get you inside."

They carried me into the house and laid me on my parents' bed while someone went for Tante Mathilde, the *traiteuse.* A jagged edge of my left collarbone poked out from a circle of swollen blue skin, and whenever anyone touched it, the faces bending over me would spin as I sank into darkness again.

People kept sticking their heads in the door and asking how I was. I saw Chance's face a few times, which only made me more miserable.

'Nonc Adolphe came in and sat on the bed. But Maman swooped on him like a hawk. "Haven't you done enough, Adolphe? *Fiche-nous la paix*—just leave us alone."

He left.

Paulo slunk around to the far wall and stared at me, his eyes red and swollen.

I wondered where my fiddle was.

At last Tante Mathilde arrived, and what happened next I'd just as soon forget. She gave me a dose of some bitter syrup that tasted like mud and made me feel as if I were floating above the bed. But I was brought back to earth real quick when Monsieur Vidrine held down my legs and Papa held me up for Tante Mathilde to set the break. I felt my bones grind together and heard the *snap* they made as the two pieces of my collarbone found each other again.

Tante Mathilde held me as I threw up. Then she applied a thick poultice of comfrey leaves, instructing Maman to change it every day to help my bones knit back together.

When she'd wrapped me tightly in strips of cloth, around my shoulders, under my arms, and across my chest, I could barely breathe. The pressure on my collarbone was so relentless that I wanted to scream. But Tante Mathilde gave me something to make me sleep, and I sank into oblivion.

And that was the end of many things.

I woke up the next morning in my parents' bed, my body a mass of pain and sickness. My collarbone screamed with pain, and my head hurt as much from the whiskey as from the fall. The morning light pierced my eyes, and my mouth felt drier than a snake's belly. I wished someone would go ahead and put me out of my misery.

I heard Tante Mathilde arrive, then her face appeared next to Maman's in the doorway. She'd already been to church to get her Ash Wednesday ashes, which stood out in a smudged cross on her forehead. "You know, Marie," she said, putting her arm around Maman's shoulders, "a mother makes her children, but not her children's hearts."

Maman turned away a dejected face. Pulling off her black shawl, Tante Mathilde set her tapestry bag full of musty-smelling jars and bottles on the floor beside the bed and sat down. After she'd examined me, she shook her head. "Eh, Félix," she said, "you fixed yourself up good this time, didn't you?"

I nodded.

"Don't you know that if you play with fire," she said, "you'll burn your shirt?"

I tried to shrug, causing the pain to stab through my shoulder. I wasn't in the mood for a lecture.

"Let's see what we can do for you." Tante Mathilde began her treatment—what some people might call faith healing—by making a large cross in the air. Then she laid her forefinger on my neck above the broken bone and traced a small cross, saying, "In the name of the Father and the Son and the Holy Ghost." Without lifting her finger, she went down my shoulder to the right and traced another, repeating the invocation the whole time. She made a third cross on the left side, then traced over the first one so that she had surrounded the break.

Kneeling beside the bed, she clasped her hands together and squeezed her eyes shut. She prayed over me for a long time, her lips moving but no sound coming out.

At last she crossed herself and rose. Reaching in her pocket, she pulled out a tiny muslin bag tied onto a string. She began knotting the string in different places. "Here's some herbs and prayers to help you get better," she said, putting it around my neck and making the sign of the cross. "You ask *le bon Dieu* to bless you every day, and wear this till it falls off the string. Then you'll be nearly good as new."

"Yes, ma'am," I said. The bag gave off a sharp, earthy smell.

Tante Mathilde passed her hand over my forehead and smiled. "Now let's change that poultice."

She lifted the limp leaves off my collarbone and pressed on a fresh batch, saying, "So, I hear you wanted to make yourself a fiddler."

I looked out the window, gritting my teeth.

"That's a big job, *mon petit,*" she persisted. "Don't you know you got to wait till you're ready for big things like that?"

"I *am* ready," I said, sounding even to myself like a stubborn child.

"Hmm, I don't know 'bout that. This shoulder don't look like it wants to be fiddling anytime soon." She rubbed some salve into the scrapes on my face and patted my hand.

"You see," she said in a voice so gentle it made me want to cry, "music's a powerful force. It can make people fall in love, fall out of love, make them happy, make them sad—all sorts of crazy things. Look what it's already done to you!" She chuckled, then poked a finger at me. "The one who plays it has to be ready."

"I don't know what you're talking about," I said.

"I know you don't, and that's why you're not ready. You ask your 'Nonc Adolphe about that. You'll see."

For a second I felt the anger rising in my chest. But then Tante Mathilde leaned over close to my face and said, "But you know what? Your will is strong. Just you wait and see."

I watched her walk out the door, her words swirling around and settling into the gloom of my world.

The next few days were one long nightmare. The torn muscles in my back and shoulder would seize up in the middle of the night with terrible spasms. Maman or Papa would have to lift me into a sitting position and rub them with liniment before they'd stop jumping. My right ankle was sprained and swollen, and the pain from the broken collarbone never ever let up.

I slept most of the time except when the pain woke me. Maman hovered and fussed over me till I dared to think maybe she'd forgiven me. And always lurking around the edges of my foggy brain was the question I didn't dare ask—"What happened to my fiddle?"

Chance showed up one afternoon with some cookies that his mama had made for me. I was so happy to see his good old face that I couldn't think what to say.

He stood around staring at the floor until finally he glared at me, his eyes flashing. "If I'm your best friend," he said, "how come you never told me about that fiddle of yours?"

A flush of embarrassment spread through me. "'Cause I didn't know if it would be any good, or if I'd really be able to play it. And then, when you got a real accordion, I was so jealous—"

Chance interrupted, "I'm sick of hearing stuff like that, Félix." He stalked around the room. "It's not *my* fault my daddy made a lot of money, you know! And if it makes you feel any better, he just *lost* a whole pile of it. He's even saying we might have to sell Maman's Chevrolet. So there. I guess you'll be happy now."

I stared in disbelief. "Of course not! I'm sorry, I really am."

Chance jabbed his finger at me. "I'm not the one

who's changed, you know. It's *you* who's making a big deal about Papa's money, not me. I try to share it with you, but no, you never even let me buy you a soda."

I ducked my head.

He went on, "I'd rather have you for a friend any day than that stupid old accordion. I can't seem to play the darned thing, anyway—it's driving me crazy."

"And everybody else, too, I bet," I said with a grin.

Chance punched me gently in the arm, and we both burst out laughing. "I'm sorry about how I acted, I really am," I said. "I never thought about it from your side." I spit on my hand and held it out. "Best friends?"

"Best friends," he said, spitting on his hand and shaking mine.

I watched him go. If I was glad about anything, it was that I'd had that one day of glory with him, when the music flowed out of me and joined with grown men, making me part of something bigger than I could ever be all by myself. I knew I'd carry that feeling to my grave.

On the first day I could get up by myself, I hobbled out into the kitchen to sit by the fire, my arm resting in a sling.

Maman was hulling rice in the hewn-log mortar near the stove, pounding and twisting the wooden pestle in a rhythmic *boom, swish, boom, swish.* Outside, the sun shone so brightly it hurt my eyes. Maman tucked a shawl around my shoulders and poured me a cup of warm milk before she let the ax fall.

"I've been waiting for you to get well enough to talk about it," she said.

Blood drummed in my ears.

Maman crossed her arms over her chest. Gone was the look of concern from her face. "So?"

My breath caught in my chest. "It was a fiddle I made out of a cigar box." My voice sounded timid and puny.

"A fiddle? Did you say a *fiddle?*" said Maman, hovering over me like a vulture. "But you were forbidden to have anything to do with fiddles, weren't you?" Her voice rose with pent-up anger.

"You deliberately defied both me and your father." Outrage showed in every line of her face.

Even a criminal is supposed to have his day in court, and I was determined to have mine. "Maman, it's not fair, it just ain't fair for you to tell me I can't play the fiddle. I've got music in my blood, just like 'Nonc Adolphe and Grandpapa, no matter what you say." My lips trembled, but I couldn't stop the words. "Besides," I said, "even *you* did something you weren't supposed to when you were young."

Maman's mouth dropped open. I'd never spoken to her like that before. "Yes," she said in a voice like a cast-iron skillet, "and I paid dearly for it. Just as you will. Now get back to bed."

"But, Maman . . ."

"You've said enough. *Va-t'en!*"

I pushed myself up and limped back to bed.

Some time later the kitchen door banged. It was Paulo, home from school. He came in to see me as usual, his cheeks flushed from the sun. I motioned him over to the bed.

"Paulo," I whispered, "do you know what they did with my fiddle?"

His eyes dropped to the floor and he nodded.

"What?" I said.

He swallowed hard before he said, "Maman burned it in the fireplace."

I threw a look at the ceiling, then clenched my eyes to shut out the image of the hungry flames licking at the varnished wood, at the scroll, at the pegs. Turning to ashes what I'd worked so hard to make. I knew a part of me had gone up in smoke along with it.

Hot tears squeezed out of the corners of my eyes. It was more than I could stand.

"I'm sorry, Félix," said Paulo, and he was crying, too. "I never meant for anything like that to happen. It's just that Maman and Papa like you so much better'n me, I wanted them to be mad at you. . . ."

"What the devil are you talking about?"

"They give you all those important jobs, and talk to you like you're a man," he said. "And Papa takes you hunting. All they ever say to me is, 'Hush, Paulo.' 'Finish your supper, Paulo.' 'Wash your hands, Paulo.'" His head drooped. "But I didn't know you'd fall out of the wagon and get all banged up and lose your fiddle."

It still wasn't making any sense. "So what have *you* got to be sorry about?"

He stared at the floor. "Maman made me tell her," he stammered. "She was so mad when you snuck out Mardi Gras morning."

I raised my head to glare at him. "She made you tell her what?"

"About your fiddle. I saw you leave with it." Paulo was sobbing now. "I'm sorry," he blubbered. "But you promised I could be in your band. You were supposed to take me with you. . . ."

"What?" I felt a crazy laugh rising at the absurdity of it. But I pushed it down, wishing instead I could shake him till his head rattled. I stared at a crack in the ceiling. "You dirty little traitor," I said at last, my voice low and mean. "My own brother."

He sobbed louder.

"Get out of here," I said. "Get out! I never want to lay eyes on you again as long as I live!"

Maman appeared in the doorway and put her arms around Paulo. "Félix! Hush that talk!"

At that moment I hated them both. My fiddle was gone up in smoke, its ashes scattered to the wind. I turned my head to the wall, my chest threatening to explode.

A mockingbird started singing in the sweet olive bush outside, and I wished I had a peashooter to aim at it. I wanted to make it and the whole world disappear.

That night, for the first time in my life, I heard Maman and Papa arguing. At first it was just muffled murmurs. But then Papa raised his voice and said, "You're being too hard on the boy, Marie."

Maman's voice, angry, said something I couldn't hear.

"Let up a little, won't you?" said Papa. "He's doing enough suffering, even if he's not willing to admit it yet. You got your way—he won't be fiddling anymore."

I put a pillow over my ears.

Next morning Maman pronounced her sentence: I would not be allowed to leave the house except for school and farmwork and chores, whenever my collarbone healed enough to do those. And nobody could visit me, not even Chance, my best friend.

I was in prison.

Penance

Maman barely spoke to me after that, her face stuck in a deep frown. She tended to me when she had to, but otherwise I might as well have been invisible.

I was sitting in the kitchen rocker on Sunday afternoon, poking at the fire with a stick in my good hand, when 'Nonc Adolphe showed up. He looked so different that I hardly recognized him, dressed in overalls and a dirty old shirt, with a straw hat on his head. He was turning from the mysterious stranger from the outside world into a farmer like everyone else.

Papa opened the door, but Maman flared up at the sight of him.

"How dare you show your face at my door!" she said, her voice shrill. "You are not welcome in my house."

"Marie," said 'Nonc, his hat in his hand, "won't you listen to me? It's not what you think."

Maman's head was shaking, but Papa stepped back and said, "Come in, Adolphe."

"Are you happy now?" said Maman. "You've taken my child away from me, with your whiskey and your music. Have you come to get Paulo, too?"

'Nonc drew back like he'd been slapped. "Marie, I didn't know nothing about it, I swear. Félix asked me if I'd teach him to play the fiddle, and I told him no because I knew you wouldn't like it. The boy made that fiddle all by himself. . . ."

"It's true, Maman," I said.

Maman held up her hand. "You've brainwashed him till he wants to be just like you. You were sitting there right across from him in that wagon—and you're going to tell me you didn't know it was him?" She gave a harsh laugh.

'Nonc Adolphe pulled himself up and took a deep breath. His lips quivered. "I had nothing to do with him getting on that wagon, Marie, I swear."

"He fell down drunk, right there in front of everyone. But what do you care—you don't give a fig for anyone but yourself."

"*Assez*, Marie," said Papa. "That's enough."

"Félix is not the first kid to get in a little trouble on Mardi Gras," said 'Nonc Adolphe. "He's a good boy—"

Maman interrupted. "You call what he did being a 'good boy'?"

Veins stood out in 'Nonc's forehead. "You don't understand anything, do you?"

"Adolphe . . ." said Papa.

"No, André, I'm tired of having to apologize to her for who I am." 'Nonc swung his gaze back to Maman. "When the British took everything from our ancestors, our people didn't escape with much but the clothes on their backs. But the one thing they held onto through all their hardships was their songs—the songs that had come down to them from their parents and their grandparents, everyone who'd gone before them, all the way back to France. Those songs carry the heart and soul of our people."

Maman glared at him. 'Nonc straightened himself up and took a deep breath. "I know I'm no great example of what you approve of in a man, Marie. But I think God has a purpose for each and every one of us, and some of us get chosen to make music. It's a duty that we take on, not some selfish scheme we cook up for our own good."

Maman gave a little "Ha!"

"It's true," said 'Nonc. "And like it or not, God gave that boy the gift." He aimed his finger at me. "You should've heard what he could do on that little bitty fiddle, that he made all by himself. You ought to be proud of him, instead of harping on how he went about doing it."

By now Maman was trembling. "How dare you try to tell me how to raise my children!" she said. "Hear me now, Adolphe—Félix will not follow in your footsteps as long as there is a breath left in my body."

With a look at Maman's stony face, 'Nonc Adolphe dropped his hands to his sides. "I give up. You'll never understand." He turned and strode to the door, but swung back around. "And don't worry—I won't darken this door again."

'Nonc Adolphe went out into what was left of the day, slamming the door behind him.

Every year since I could remember, I'd agonized over what to give up in penance for Lent. For us Catholics it had to be something that meant enough to you to be a hardship, yet something you could stand to do without. Like meat, which we didn't touch from Mardi Gras until Easter Day.

That year around our house you'd swear we'd given up each other for Lent. The sight of Paulo never failed to conjure up a picture of my fiddle burning in the fireplace, and I couldn't bring myself to speak to him. So he mostly stayed out of my way, slinking around like a gunshy hound. Maman did her work with her face set in grim lines. Plowing time had arrived, so Papa left every morning before the sun came up and came in after dark, too tired to do anything but eat supper and go to bed.

And 'Nonc Adolphe kept his promise not to come near our house again.

As for me, music was my sacrifice, and I didn't know how I could ever make a greater one.

My body mended faster than my spirit. As the fiddle calluses peeled off my fingers, my sprains and torn muscles
healed, too. One night Tante Mathilde's muslin bag
snapped off its string and, sure enough, the constant pain
of the broken bone had eased up. I would've been able to
go back to school if it hadn't been called off for planting
season.

That night I slept upstairs in my own bed.

"G'night, Félix," said Paulo as I blew out the candle. I
turned my back on him without a word.

Maman announced it was time for me to make my confession to Père Benoît. It was the first time I'd left the
house since Mardi Gras Day. With my arm in a sling, I
took off on Henri, breathing the fresh air deep into my
lungs.

I found the aging priest planting Irish potatoes in his
garden. He squinted up at me, then plunged a trowel
deep into the soil, held the dirt to one side, and stuck a
sprouted potato half into the hole. "I'm late getting these
in the ground," he said, "but I'll just have to have faith."
He tamped the soil and goose-stepped down the row, his
black cassock streaked with muddy stains.

"So, Félix," he said, burying another potato, "I hear
you've been up to no good."

"*Oui, mon père.* I mean, *Non, mon père,*" I said, ducking my head.

His trowel scritched into the earth again before he said, "You made a fiddle, contrary to your mother's wishes?"

"Yes, Father. And I came to make my confession."

"Some say a fiddle's the instrument of the devil."

I fixed my gaze on the whitewashed walls of the church. "Why would they say that?"

"They say it leads a man astray and tempts him into evil." He looked up at me. "Are you trying to prove that theory, Félix?"

"No, sir. I don't think I did any evil."

"What have you come to confess, then?" Reaching the end of the row, he stood up, dusted off his cassock, and headed toward the back door of the church.

"That I disobeyed Maman and Papa." We entered the damp gloom of the church. "That I drank whiskey. That I ran the Mardi Gras without permission." He turned his dark-eyed gaze on me like a challenge, so I went on. "But I didn't do the work of the devil. If God is anywhere, I swear He lives in the middle of a violin."

Père Benoît stared at me in surprise. Outside, buggy wheels squelched softly past on the road, and a wren chirped by the window. I watched his nostrils flare and collapse until finally he said, "I will hear your confession."

In the safety of the confessional I told it all as best I could—how I'd heard 'Nonc Adolphe play, how Maman had forbidden me to even mention a fiddle in our house, how I'd made my fiddle, how I'd ridden on the Mardi

Gras wagon and fallen off, and how my fiddle was gone forever. Père Benoît listened without interrupting, his profile shaded by the screen between us.

When I'd told all there was to tell, he bent his head in prayer. In the end he gave me twenty Our Fathers and twenty Hail Marys every day for a month, and told me to remember to obey my father and my mother.

After giving me the final blessing, he chucked me under the chin. "You made a good case for yourself, Félix Octave LeBlanc. You'll turn out all right." I nodded and was out the door and into the warm afternoon.

When I got back to prison, I told Maman what my penance was. She didn't say a word but stirred her cornbread batter till I thought she'd beat it to death. She had probably been hoping Père Benoît would flog me with a cat-o'-nine-tails.

I knelt on the *prie-Dieu* before supper and began the twenty repetitions of the words I'd learned so long ago. Every time I got to the part about "lead us not into temptation," I saw the night of the Christmas party at Chance's and felt the first notes of 'Nonc Adolphe's fiddle sear into my heart.

That evening, sitting by the fire with the new issue of the French newspaper from Opelousas, I read about all sorts of things going on in the outside world. The Panama Canal had opened, so ships could now sail from the Pacific Ocean to the Atlantic and back again. Alexander

Graham Bell had placed a telephone call from New York City to his assistant, Mr. Watson, all the way in San Francisco. And the Germans were using mustard gas against the Allied trenches in France.

Looking at the shadowed faces of my mother, father, and brother, I thought we were living in our own war zone. The distance that separated us seemed wider than the China Sea.

As the days of Lent marched toward Easter, the world turned a bright shade of green. The newly plowed fields gave off a dusky scent full of promise. It was the first time since I could remember that I wasn't out helping Papa with the spring planting. But he said if I didn't wait till my bone finished knitting itself back together, I'd have trouble with it the rest of my life.

At first I was glad to get out of all the backbreaking work. And Papa never complained. But watching him leave early every morning and return exhausted in the evening began to leave a guilty taste in my mouth.

To my surprise I began to miss the work, too. I liked putting a tiny seed in the ground, covering it with dirt, and waiting for a green sprout to appear like magic. I knew music was in my blood, but maybe farming was, too. It seemed the whole world was busy reaching toward a common goal, and even that had been taken away from me.

I tried to help Maman plant the kitchen garden, but

with my arm still in a sling, I wasn't much help. I couldn't shoot my shotgun. The spring air pulled me outside, but there was nothing to do and nobody to do it with.

Late one morning, Maman let me out of my cage for a little while.

"Félix," she said, "your father wanted to work through dinner today. I need you to take him something to eat."

"Yes, ma'am," I said eagerly.

"But mind you come straight back." She folded a big wedge of cornbread, a boiled egg, and a potato into a cloth and handed it to me. I burst through the door and out into the open.

The sun felt good on my broken bone, although each step caused a dull bump of pain. A restlessness came over me that made me want to break into a run, down the road, past the horizons of my life and far beyond.

Papa had finished planting the Olivier acreage that we'd surrounded with our levee and had moved on to the LeBlanc farm. I saw him up ahead, bent over the harness. As I stepped into the moist dark wake where the plow had wedged open the soil, white egrets plucked at grubs and worms with their sharp beaks.

Papa looked up and watched me coming. Little white lines beside his eyes showed where he'd been squinting in the sun. "I'm surprised to see you out and about," he said. "I don't want you rushing that bone."

"Maman sent me with your dinner," I said.

Papa shook his head, licking his finger and sticking it up to check the direction of the breeze. "No time for it. The colter on the plow's got out of whack, and I want to finish this field before the weather changes." I heard the fatigue and frustration in his voice. "Félix, take ahold of Hip's head—he's getting skittish on me."

I went around and took hold of the mule's harness. Hip stuck his gray nose into my chest and closed his eyes. I stroked his thick neck. "I'm sorry I can't help you with the planting, Papa."

He went on working. A flock of ducks angled steadily toward the north.

"Can you forgive me, Papa?"

He glanced up. "Are you sorry for what you did?"

I rubbed Hip's forehead. "I'm sorry I disobeyed you. I'm sorry that I went on the wagon. I'm sorry I drank whiskey." I squinted up at the sun. "And I'm sorry I can't be a fiddle player."

Papa's hands stopped working. He looked up, straight into my eyes, and then he said the last words I ever thought I'd hear out of his mouth. "To tell you the truth," he said, "so am I."

I stared at the top of his head as he bent over the plow again. "Y-y-you are?"

He shrugged. "A little music at the end of the day lightens a man's load considerable, if you ask me."

"But, Papa . . ."

"Don't go getting any ideas, son. You still went against what we said. I told you before, it's just something you got to get over."

But how would I ever get over it?

As I trudged back toward the gloom of home, something snapped inside of me. Maman had been making me feel like Judas betraying Jesus Christ, when it turned out Papa didn't even seem to mind if I was a fiddler. But then how could he go along with Maman in making sure I never played a fiddle?

When I got home, Maman set me to stirring her *roux* on the stove. "And don't you dare let it burn," she said.

As I stirred the concoction of fat and flour that went into just about everything Maman cooked, my face burned till I could feel my eyeballs blushing. Here I was, reduced to women's work, watching the *roux* brown as if it had anything to do with anything.

With each circle the spoon made, my frustration grew. If I thought my life was dull before, it was nothing compared to this desert. I couldn't take much more.

That's when a light went on in my head, an idea so simple that I couldn't believe it hadn't occurred to me before. What if I just left? What if I went somewhere else, somewhere I could play music and be who *I* wanted to be, not who they were trying to make me be?

And before the thought had had time to settle in my brain, I knew I would do it. I would leave home.

New Orleans. I would go to New Orleans, where the Mississippi River headed for the Gulf of Mexico. Home of the Cotton Exchange, where Chance's daddy had gotten rich. Where the buildings looked like they were trimmed in lace, where the Creole food was the best in the world, and where the music didn't stop till the sun came up.

Joy washed over me. I would get there if I had to walk every step of the way.

chapter twelve

The Chosen Ones

That night I waited till the house was quiet and then waited some more before swinging my feet out of bed and lighting the candle like in my fiddle-making days. My heart beat so loud I thought it would wake Paulo the Traitor. Wrapping a change of clothes in a blanket, I crept down the stairs and into the kitchen.

A leftover wedge of cornbread, a link of sausage, and a sweet potato went into my pockets. A length of rope tied around my bundle allowed me to sling it over my good shoulder. I wished I could take my shotgun, but decided I wouldn't need it in the city. Grabbing a piece of charcoal from the fireplace and ripping a page from the Sears and Roebuck catalogue, I wrote, "Gone away to be somebody." I left the note on the table.

My hand was on the door before I had another thought.

My pocketknife lay in a carved wooden box on the mantel in my parents' room. It belonged to me. I stuck my head in their room.

Papa's heavy breathing betrayed his exhaustion, and Maman frowned even in her sleep. They lay there in the moonlight, side by side, like a brick wall I'd been butting my head against.

I'm just doing them a favor, I thought. They'll have one less mouth to feed, and one less bother in their lives. They'll probably be glad to be rid of me.

I crept to the mantel and snatched my knife, slipping its familiar weight into its old place in my pocket. Then, pulling my coat and hat off their pegs, I opened the door. "So long," I said silently, and stepped out into the night.

I had one stop to make before I left for good. I had to tell Chance goodbye.

His house shone silver in the moonlight. Picking up some pieces of oyster shell from the driveway, I went around back and lobbed them up at his window. Before long his sleepy head appeared, then disappeared; soon he opened the back door and came out in his bare feet.

"What in thunder are you doing here?" he said, his voice thick with sleep.

"I can't take it anymore at home. I'm leaving, going to New Orleans," I whispered. "I came to say goodbye."

He perked up. "What're you gonna do down there?"

"Be a musician," I said. The words hanging in the night air scared me a little.

"That's a long way to go for that," he said. "Want me

to come with you?" He didn't sound too enthusiastic.

"Naw, what've *you* got to run away from?" I said.

"Why don't you stay here? I can hide you in the barn and smuggle your meals out to you. Then you can teach me some music."

His sleepy grin was so catching that I was almost tempted to take him up on it. But I was tired of hiding. "Naw," I said, "I got to go find a place where I don't have to be ashamed to be who I am."

He shrugged. "I hate to see you go. You got any money?"

I shook my head.

"Wait here." Chance disappeared inside and soon reappeared. He grabbed my hand and slapped a coin into it. Large and cool, it glinted in the moonlight. It was a ten-dollar gold piece! "My grandma gave it to me for Christmas," he said.

"No, Chance, I can't take that."

"Yes, you can. I don't want to be reading in the *Times-Picayune* that a Cajun boy from L'Anse Rougeau starved to death on the streets of New Orleans. You got food?"

I nodded. "Thanks, Chance . . . I don't know what to say."

Chance grinned. "You just said it. Now go on, get outta here before you get caught." He grabbed me in a bear hug that nearly smothered me, then spit on his hand. "Best friends?"

"Best friends," I choked out. I had to turn away before he saw the tears in my eyes.

I walked away, leaving behind my only friend in the world.

Soon I was following the road toward Eunice. From there I could hit the road east, maybe even hop a train. A damp chill settled over the fields, and thunder rumbled in the distance. I set one foot in front of the other, over and over again, my collarbone throbbing with each step, until home was far behind me.

New Orleans and all its possibilities lay ahead. And Chance's ten-dollar gold coin in my pocket bumped my leg with every step. Why, that was enough to buy myself a fiddle, and have some left over to live off of till I could make some money playing. How could I have been so wrong about his friendship? Just stupid, I guessed.

The whoosh of wings close by my head startled me out of my thoughts. An owl. Swift-moving clouds covered the moon so that I couldn't see my hand in front of my face.

Each step took me farther away from everything I'd ever known—Maman, Papa, Paulo, Chance, all the folks in L'Anse Rougeau. That was all behind me now. I was free.

Coyotes yipped a wild chorus, sending a quick shiver up my back. But then I laughed at myself and joined in their howling, pushing forward into the thick darkness as if I was the only human being alive on the face of the earth.

I'd been walking into the dead of the night for a long time when the first fat raindrop plopped onto my skin. Another followed, and another until, within moments, they joined together into a solid sheet of rain. My clothes quickly got soaked through. Thunder crashed all around, as if I were on the inside of some huge bass drum.

Every step became a struggle as I sloshed through the road that had suddenly turned to a muddy wash. My bundle weighed down my good shoulder and pulled on my broken collarbone, which had begun to throb with pain. The cold rain dripped off my hat and down my neck, and heavy gusts of wind blew the water into my eyes.

A flash of lightning struck a hackberry tree not fifty feet ahead, and the air exploded in an earsplitting peal of thunder. Fear launched me into the soggy ditch beside the road, where I sank to my knees in cold, mucky water.

I covered my head and waited for the world to end. But when it didn't, I got the courage to look up. Even through the driving rain, I could hear the sizzle and smell the smoke of the fried tree. I crossed myself and thanked God for sparing me.

My ears still ringing, I looked off to the left up ahead.

The lightning had revealed a tiny shack in the middle of an overgrown field. Step by mushy step, I felt my way along the short lane leading to it. I didn't care who lived there, as long as I got out of the storm.

Blackberry vines choked the tiny porch. I'd never appreciated a roof so much as when that rain stopped pounding on my head. At my knock, the door fell forward, dangling on one leather hinge.

"Hello? Anyone home?" I called. No answer. I pushed into the one-room shack.

Another flash of lightning lit up my dingy shelter. An iron bed frame leaned against the wall, the contents of its mattress spilling out and padding the rats' nests in the corners. A rusty pile of empty tin cans teetered beside a small cookstove, and the leaky roof dribbled puddles onto the floor. Still, compared to the outdoors, I'd found a palace.

As my eyes adjusted to the gloom, I hung my soggy jacket and hat on a peg, then scoped out the driest spot on the bed to sit on. Every stitch of my clothing was soaked through, and I began to shiver uncontrollably. Thinking that maybe some food would warm me, I pulled out the squashed potato and sausage and gobbled them down, topped off with a pocketful of damp cornbread crumbs. Feeling a little better, I leaned back against the wall and closed my eyes, sighing heavily. My knees still shook, and the pain in my shoulder was wide awake.

I lay there in limbo, forcing my mind not to think. I was about to drift off when something startled me out of my daydream—the sound of a heavy footstep on the porch.

Tales of Madame Grands-Doigts raced through my mind as I sat bolt upright, my heart in my throat.

I'd never felt real fear before, the kind that zings through your body and makes you sick at your stomach, the kind that makes the back of your neck crawl like a nest of cockroaches. Every muscle in my body pulled taut as a fiddle string. I thought of the knife in my pocket but didn't dare move.

The door swung forward on its one hinge, and a flash of distant lightning illuminated the figure of a man. I opened my mouth but could force no sound to come out.

I heard a *scritch,* and a match flared. The man was dressed in a long black coat, his dripping hat pulled low over his eyes. I pressed myself into the wall behind me.

The match went out, plunging the room into sudden darkness. He lit another one. "Someone there?" said a wary voice. The match came closer.

"Yeah," I said in a voice barely above a whisper.

A third match was lit, so close I could smell its sulfurous fumes. Then came a deep, throaty laugh that I thought for sure was the sound of a murderer.

"Well, would you look who's here?"

The hat came off, and there stood 'Nonc Adolphe.

Relief so keen flooded through me that I thought I'd pass out. I jumped up and just barely kept from throwing my arms around his neck. "'Nonc Adolphe, it's you!"

"What the devil are you doing way out here on a night like this, Stretch?" he said. "You nearly gave me a heart attack!"

"Me?" I said, finally catching my breath. "What about you?"

'Nonc slung a knapsack off his back, along with an oilcloth bag holding the outline of a fiddle case. Digging into the knapsack, he pulled out a candle, which he lit in an old tin can on top of the stove. His glance took in my bundle and my coat and hat. "Looks like we're both running away from home, eh, '*ti boy*?"

"Y-y-you, too?" I couldn't believe my ears. "But it's right in the middle of planting."

'Nonc shrugged. "No time like the present." He pulled off his duster, the same one he'd worn at Mardi Gras, and hung it next to my coat. "Besides, look who's talking."

"Yeah, but I can't help Papa because of my arm. All I do is sit around the house doing women's work and looking at Maman frowning at me. Her and Paulo, the little snitch who got me into all this trouble. It was driving me crazy."

'Nonc pulled yellowed paper and sticks from a box behind the stove and soon had a little blaze going. "How you figure it's Paulo's fault?"

I sat at the foot of the bed where I could stretch out

my cold fingers to the heat. "He's the one who told Maman about my fiddle," I said.

'Nonc dusted off a hide-bottomed chair and sat down to roll himself a cigarette. He lit it off the candle and fixed his gaze on me. "As I recall," he said, "you fell off that wagon all by yourself. And when they took off your mask, everybody saw it was you. Seems to me your Maman was going to find out anyhow."

"Well, still . . . you taking his side?"

"I'm not taking anybody's side. I just can't stomach a man who don't take responsibility for his own actions."

"Like you, you mean?" Irritation rose in my throat. I didn't come all this way to get lectured to by another grownup.

'Nonc smoked in silence for a while. The thunder moved off into the distance, the wind died down, and the storm settled into a steady downpour.

"So what's your plan, Stretch?" he said at last.

"I'm going to New Orleans," I said, my enthusiasm rising again. "I got ten dollars of Chance's in my pocket, and I'm gonna buy me a fiddle first thing. Then I'm going to be a musician."

'Nonc smiled a haggard smile. "Just like that, huh?"

"Well, yeah. 'Where the music never stops till the sun comes up.' And like you told Maman, I'm one of the ones God chose to make music."

"That's true, I did say that." 'Nonc leaned his chair

back against the wall. "But that don't mean you gotta go all the way to New Orleans to do it. Besides, you ever hear of paying your dues?"

"What d'you mean?"

"It's sort of like a crop—you don't just go straight to the harvest. You got to plow and plant and tend and hoe and do all kinds of work before it pays off. Farmers and musicians pay more dues than anybody, if you ask me."

"I already played on the Mardi Gras wagon," I said defiantly.

"Yep, and a fine job you did, too," said 'Nonc. "But playing with a bunch of drunked-up country folks is a far sight from making a living on the streets of New Orleans. That's a rough town."

"I don't care," I said, sticking out my chin. "I'll get a job if I have to."

"You need to go back home, Stretch," he said, like he was pronouncing a sentence.

"Don't *you* start telling me what to do, too!" I shouted, punching the soggy mattress.

"I'm only trying to tell you for your own good." 'Nonc cupped his hand under a steady drip from the ceiling. "You see, the problem with leaving home is that you can never really go back again—at least, not to the way it was. You gotta be ready to leave it all behind, and I'm not so sure I'd recommend that. Being homeless is a mighty lonesome way to live."

"If nobody ever left home, no one would ever get any-where," I said. 'Nonc was making me tired.

"Take it from me, Stretch," he said, sounding weary himself, "the big wide world ain't always all it's cracked up to be. Sometimes what you're looking for is right under your nose, if you'd only open your eyes and see it."

I leaned toward him. "Oh, yeah? Then how come you're taking off again?"

'Nonc stared at the floor a long time before he answered. "I was reading the newspaper tonight, and I saw an ad for a job that's maybe more up my alley."

"What kind of job?" I asked.

"It don't matter. The truth is, the road's got ahold of me and won't let go. I thought I could come back and do what they wanted me to, be who they wanted me to be. But it's just not in me." He looked at the rain pelting the window. "I've got to get out while I still can, even though it kills me to know what your mama will think of me."

"So you know how I feel," I said.

'Nonc sighed. "Don't say I didn't warn you." He stood abruptly and tossed me a dry shirt from his rucksack. "We sure picked a fine night for traveling, eh, Stretch? Here, you better put this on. I'm going to unsaddle Gypsy." He threw on his coat and stepped back out into the rain.

I peeled off my wet shirt and pulled on 'Nonc's. The dry cotton felt like a warm hug—and I hadn't had many of those lately. Suddenly overcome with weariness, I stretched out on what was left of the damp mattress.

'Nonc brought in a leather-wrapped bedroll and laid it on the floor near the stove. Within minutes he was snoring softly, leaving me alone again.

chapter thirteen

Six Sides to a Brick

Sometimes when you're the most tired, it's hardest to fall asleep. Fleas in the moss mattress began having me for a picnic, and rain plopped around me through the roof. It was like trying to sleep in a leaky boat.

And that got me to thinking about the levee, and all those tiny cottonseeds that would've begun to sprout by now. If the water got into that field, the crop would be lost, along with all Papa's hard work and the money he'd paid for the seed. There wasn't enough money to buy new seed.

The bayou would be rising higher by the minute, licking slowly away at all that dirt we'd piled there, shovel by heavy shovelful, all winter long. A queasy feeling shifted around in the pit of my stomach.

My collarbone throbbed, and I ached all the way down my back and my arm. I clawed at the fleas biting my neck, my back, my ankle. Flipping over and clamping my hands over my ears, I tried to shut out the snorts and snores coming from 'Nonc Adolphe, and the drone of the endless water falling out of the sky.

My eyes clenched shut, and I sank into a nervous limbo filled with flitting shadows. My grandpapa Olivier held his fiddle and seemed to glare at me with a look full of reproach. My LeBlanc uncles and aunts and grandparents and great-grandparents all the way back to *Acadie* gathered around to stare. They said nothing, but behind them were the fields they had worked for generations. Papa labored out there in the distance, his back hunched under the heavy burden of his life.

None of them would go away and leave me alone through that long night. When I felt a hand on my shoulder, I cried out and sat up, ready to fend off another soggy ghost.

"Rise and shine, Stretch—New Orleans awaits." It was 'Nonc Adolphe.

I rubbed my eyes and scratched at my fleabites. Through the dingy window, I saw the rain still falling.

"Papa's levee won't hold through all this," I said.

"Most likely not," said 'Nonc. "But that's not our problem anymore, is it?"

I looked up at him, trying to see if he could really be so casual about it. And just like that, I knew what I had to do.

I jumped out of my flea-ridden bed. "We gotta go back, 'Nonc. Papa can't do it by himself."

'Nonc looked out at the gray dawn. "Good for you," he said. "That way your mama's heart won't get broken twice in the same day."

"But 'Nonc, you gotta come, too. Papa'll be desperate."

"I can't go back," he said, as if to himself. "I already tried that."

I glared at him in disbelief. He wouldn't look me in the eye. Instead, he went to his coat and pulled out a small leather packet.

"Here," he said, shoving it into my hands. "I'd intended to mail this. But since you're going back, you can take it with you."

"What is it?"

"Just give it to your mother with my love. Tell her I'm sorry I always let her down. And try to convince her that I didn't put you up to running away—she'll never believe it, though."

I nodded and tucked the packet into my soggy jacket.

He pulled on his coat and hat and shouldered his knapsack. Picking up his fiddle, he held it for half a second before pushing it toward me. "And here," he said, "you'll be needing one of these—to remember me by."

My mouth fell open. "Naw, 'Nonc, I can't take your fiddle."

"Go on," he said, his voice thick. "Your grandpapa would want you to have it—especially since you're the one staying home. I've been thinking of getting me a new one anyway." I knew that wasn't true. "Just do right by it, you hear?"

There wasn't anything to say; all I could do was nod. He turned and strode out the door.

I set the fiddle down and reached in my pocket for Chance's ten-dollar coin. "'Nonc, wait!" I called, and ran after him.

I threw my arms around him. "Thank you, 'Nonc. Thank you! I'll never forget you."

Before he stepped back, I slipped the gold coin into his coat pocket.

The rain had let up a little. As he rode away, it made me feel good to think of that shiny weight hiding in his coat for him to discover later. I hoped he would use it on a new fiddle. I'd have plenty of time to pay Chance back later.

Back inside, I took a step toward the oilcloth sack, toward my fortune or my doom, I didn't know which. I swung open the case like a magic door.

And there it lay. 'Nonc's fiddle, my grandfather's fiddle. *My* fiddle.

I was afraid to touch it for fear it would disappear, dissolve into dust like the white powder left behind by the rosin on 'Nonc's bow. I squatted there staring at it, trying to think what it meant.

It meant facing Maman if I went back, and starting up the whole war all over again. Or else it meant I could go on to New Orleans and be a real musician like I'd planned.

I saw myself standing on a corner of Jackson Square, between St. Louis Cathedral and the Mississippi River. I saw an admiring crowd clapping and throwing me money. I looked for familiar faces, but there were none. And I felt the weight of a guilt I carried inside of me, the same one that had brought 'Nonc Adolphe back to try to turn himself into a farmer.

I rocked back and forth on my heels, finally reaching out and plucking a string. The old feeling peeked in, the sheer joy of playing music. But just then the rain picked up again, drumming harder on the roof and dribbling on the floor.

I closed the case and slipped it into its waterproof bag. Then I pulled on my still-wet jacket, buttoned it around the fiddle, and stepped out into the downpour.

I set out through the steady rain, clutching the treasured sack to my chest and feeling like I'd never be dry again. There seemed to be twice as many steps on the way back, each and every slippery one filled with urgency and dread.

Finally, I neared the cotton field. The rain beat on my hat and down my face. But through it I could see figures in the distance, one, two—yes, three people working on the levee. I broke into a lame trot between two high rows of cotton, where an endless line of tiny sprouts were taking a pounding from the rain.

The wagon stood under a tree a ways off, and there I went first to tuck my fiddle under the seat. Then I ran to join my father, my mother, and my little brother.

With the noise of the rain and their concentration, they didn't notice me. On the other side of the levee, the bayou lapped close to the top of our dirt wall. I touched Paulo's shoulder and pulled the shovel he was struggling with from his muddy hands.

"Félix! It's you!" he cried. Nearby, Maman swung her head at me. For a moment she just stared. Then she dropped her shovel and waded toward me, finally putting her arms around my shoulders and pulling me to her. "You came back," she said. I looked at her mud-streaked face and thought I saw tears amidst the raindrops.

Papa, looking like some boggy swamp creature, showed his white teeth in the gloom. "It's seeping in underneath the levee," he shouted against the pounding rain. "We're trying to shore it up wherever it leaks through."

I nodded and began shoveling heavy scoops of mud onto the levee, which had shrunk to half of what we'd built. Paulo dropped to his knees and pushed armfuls of muck at ground level.

I plopped scoop after scoop of mud onto the levee,

ignoring the ache in my collarbone. On and on we bat-
tled the water that seemed to be taking over the world. It
came from above, it came from below, and it leered at us
over the top of the levee until I thought it would dissolve
us all.

But gradually, almost without us noticing, the rain
slacked. One minute we were in a liquid world, and suddenly we were surrounded by air again. A sliver of blue
sky winked at us from the far horizon.

Papa stopped for the first time since I'd arrived and
squinted at the sky. He looked in all directions. Then he
threw his shovel to the ground, ripped his limp straw hat
off his head, and hurled it at the sky. "Ay-ee! We did it!"
he shouted, flashing a smile to rival the invisible sun.

"We did it!" yelled Paulo, trying to hop up and down
against the mud that sucked at his feet. To my astonish-
ment, Maman even let out a whoop, followed by a long,
throaty laugh.

I couldn't help but join in the muddy family embrace.
Then I reached down and grabbed a handful of mud, lob-
bing it at Paulo and hitting him square in the chest. He
stared in surprise before pitching a blob back at me,
catching me in the stomach. Papa reached down and
added his contribution, until we had a full-fledged mud
fight going on. Maman stood by, laughing and clapping
like a young girl.

Tante Mathilde, who'd been waiting at home, filled the bathtub with hot water and made us bathe before we could come in the house. When the sun burst through the clouds, we all shouted and waved as if an old friend had returned from a long absence.

It wasn't until I sat down to the breakfast Tante had cooked that I realized how badly my shoulder was hurting. I couldn't use my left hand. Maman tied it up in a dish-towel sling and handed me a cup of coffee milk with extra sugar.

We ate in ravenous silence, exhaustion beginning to take the place of our excitement. I couldn't wait to crawl into my own, flea-free bed.

But first I had some explaining to do.

"I was running away to New Orleans," I said suddenly. Everyone stopped chewing and looked at me. I took a deep breath and went on, "I thought that was the right thing to do. But it wasn't, and I'm glad I came back."

Papa looked at Maman and took a swig of coffee. "We're glad you came back, too, Félix."

"*I'm* glad you came back," said Paulo, leaning his head on my shoulder for a second.

"Well, it was the storm that stopped me. After I nearly got struck by lightning, I stopped in a little shack. And believe it or not, 'Nonc Adolphe showed up there, too."

Maman's face drew down in her usual frown.

"He said you wouldn't believe it," I said urgently, "but

it's true. It was a coincidence. He was leaving for New Orleans, too."

Maman gasped and threw her hand over her mouth. Papa set down his cup. "Adolphe is gone?"

I nodded. "Maman, he said to tell you he's sorry he always disappoints you. He said it killed him to know what you would think of him, but the road had ahold of him and wouldn't let him go, and he couldn't be who you wanted him to be." My words hung over the table, changing our lives. I got up and pulled the packet out of my coat. "And he said to give you this."

Maman took the water-stained packet from me. She looked at it for a minute before untying the lace that held it closed. Her hand went back to her mouth, and as she looked at Papa, her eyes filled with fat tears. "André," she whispered, "he's given us the house and his land."

She put her head down in the crook of her elbow, and her shoulders shook with sobs.

Paulo and I sat frozen. I couldn't remember ever seeing Maman cry, unless you counted earlier when she first saw me, but I couldn't be sure of that. Papa got up and put his arms around her.

"I didn't want *that*," she wept. "I just wanted him to come back. He's the only family I have left. I've lost my brother."

"You got to watch what you wish for," said Tante Mathilde quietly.

Paulo's bottom lip quivered. I stood up and took him by the hand. "Come on, PeeWee," I said, "let's go get some rest." He looked up at me in adoration.

At the door, I turned back. "Oh, and he gave me his fiddle."

Late-afternoon light streamed through the window when I opened my eyes. My first thought was of 'Nonc's fiddle under the wagon seat. I tried to sit up, but pain shot through me. I decided instead to lie there and enjoy the cool of the sheets that Maman had woven from the cotton we grew. No store-bought sheets could have felt better.

Paulo was still sleeping, his arm thrown over his face. When I looked for the anger that had been riding around inside of me, I found it was gone.

Maybe I shouldn't have given him something to tell on me about.

Muffled voices rose up from Maman and Papa's bedroom. If I stayed in bed forever, I would never know what they were talking about.

Finally, I had to know what was going on. I limped downstairs.

Tante Mathilde was in the kitchen stirring a big pot of gumbo. She took one look at me and ladled some into a bowl, which she set in front of me with a hot biscuit.

"Here you go, Stretch," she said with a glint in her

eye. Wondering where she'd heard 'Nonc's nickname for me, I slathered the biscuit with butter and muscadine jelly and popped it whole into my mouth.

"Good," I mumbled.

"I had to make myself useful," said Tante Mathilde. "Your mama was doing enough praying for the both of us."

I was gulping spoonfuls of gumbo when Maman came out of the bedroom, her eyes red and puffy. Papa stood behind her as she sat across the table and took my hand.

"I thought you were gone for good, Félix," she said. "I couldn't bear it if both you *and* Adolphe had gone away." She choked back tears.

I stared at her, not daring to swallow my mouthful of rice and gumbo.

"We found your note this morning, on the way out to the cotton field. I couldn't think of anything else the whole time we were fighting the rain." She drew a ragged breath. "And for the first time, I began to see your side of things. I thought back to what it was like to be your age, to want something so bad that you'll go against your parents. And I realized that the very thing I was afraid of—that if you learned to play music, you'd shirk your responsibilities instead of staying on the farm and helping us—well, that's the very thing I forced you to do."

Tante Mathilde set dishes of bread pudding in front of

us. "There's six sides to every brick," she said. Maman shot her an exasperated look.

"I thought about my own papa," she went on, "and how hard he worked on the farm, and how happy he was when he could finally sit on the porch at the end of the day and play that sweet, sweet music." She turned my hand over and rubbed my fingertips where the calluses used to be. "You have his hands. I guess Adolphe was right, you *do* have music in your blood. And maybe I was wrong to stand in your way."

Staring into her blue eyes, I saw for the first time how I'd caused my share of trouble and pain for her. Sure enough, I'd done the very thing she was afraid fiddling would make me do. I dropped my gaze, and found myself meaning it when I said, "I'm sorry, too, Maman. For sneaking around and disobeying you."

"Maybe we can start over?" she said.

"Yes, ma'am." I threw my good arm around her.

She pushed her chair back and stood up. "So," she said brightly, "where is that famous fiddle?"

I swallowed. "Out in the wagon."

"It's right here," said Papa. "I found it this morning." He pulled it out from behind the *garde-manger.*

"Could you play us a tune?" said Maman. "I wouldn't mind some cheering up." She disappeared into the bedroom.

I sat frozen in my chair, not trusting my ears.

Papa put the fiddle on the table in front of me. "Come on, son, show us what you can do."

I laid a trembling hand on the fiddle case that held the wooden box strung up with quiet strings.

Paulo appeared in the doorway, rubbing the sleep from his eyes. "What's going on?" he said.

Opening the case, I picked up the fiddle. It was big compared to my cigar-box one, yet it felt like it had always lived in my hands. Hesitantly, I tuned it up, then set it on my sore shoulder and picked up the bow. Though its weight sent a stabbing pain through my left side, you couldn't have stopped me for all the gold coins in the world.

I wasn't sure my fingers remembered what to do, and I scraped around on the strings for a while, my cheeks stinging. I hunted for the notes of Maman's old favorite, *"La Valse du Bayou."*

As the music started to flow, Papa and Tante Mathilde gaped at me, looks of wonder on their faces. Then Papa looked up and stared, and I followed his gaze.

There in the doorway stood Maman, a mischievous smile on her face and that crazy black velvet hat, the Parisian Gainsborough, on her head. Its crushed velvet roses sagged around her face.

Papa grinned and held out his hand to her. She took it, and they began to step together in wide circles around the kitchen. Tante Mathilde grabbed Paulo's hand and pulled him along to her lively steps, making us all laugh.

I was making them dance, me and this fiddle of mine.

The sound of merriment filled the corners of the room and began to chase away the long sadness.

chapter fourteen

Housewarming

The church overflowed with colorful Easter hats and dresses; and uncomfortable suits and shoes. Chance tugged at his stiff collar when I passed his pew and gave him a wave. I had to smile, remembering how his eyes had bugged out when I told him about the night I'd run away and how I finally got my fiddle.

It seemed Père Benoît deliberately stretched out the homily just because we were all so hungry. The thought of the *cochon de lait* we'd left cooking in a deep pit at home made me drool like a mad dog. I remembered the last meat I'd eaten, back on Mardi Gras day, when I still had my cigar-box fiddle, when Maman didn't know anything about it, when I wasn't speaking to Chance. I felt like I'd aged ten years since then.

At last Communion was taken, the final hymn and prayer were done, and we spilled out of the stuffy church like chickens at feeding time.

"You wanna ride with us?" said Chance, waving at the red Chevrolet.

156

"Sure!" I climbed into the rumble seat behind the big family of Guidrys. The magic carriage rolled along like a feather pillow. Chance pulled out a big bag of jellybeans, and shared them even-steven with me.

It still took me by surprise every time we turned off from our usual route home and headed toward 'Nonc Adolphe's—our—place. In the week since we'd moved in, Maman had wandered from room to room, touching the furniture and the walls like she was seeing her childhood home for the first time.

We pulled into the yard, under the ancient live oaks my great-great-grandmother had planted. Azalea bushes bloomed a pink so bright it hurt your eyes, and white dogwood blossoms drifted down on the breeze. 'Nonc Adolphe had left the place looking like new, and all we'd had to do was move in our belongings. 'Nonc Louis was buying our old house and land for his son, who was about to get married. Papa would get a cash payment every month till it was paid off.

Papa pulled up in the wagon behind us. Maman wore a new dress the color of a bluejay's wings, and when she smiled at us, the corners of her mouth turned up all the way.

I unhitched the wagon while Chance and Monsieur Guidry helped Papa pull up the meat from the pit. There was a suckling pig, a goat, and a lamb, along with a huge ham from Tante Mathilde. Papa began slicing the meat and heaping it onto platters and plates. Each friend and relative who arrived added more food to the long tables set up under the trees. My tastebuds welcomed that meat like a rainstorm after a drought.

As soon as we'd stuffed ourselves, all us kids got out our Easter eggs to *pâquer*. We'd choose a partner, and tap the ends of our boiled eggs together until one of them cracked. Whoever's egg didn't break won the round. I had a special hold and a secret spot that made my egg a winner, until I took on Chance and his guinea egg. It wasn't long before he'd beaten the socks off all of us.

After that his mama passed out gold foil–wrapped chocolate eggs, declaring each and every one of us a winner. She pinched my cheek. "How do you like your new house?" she said from under her flowered Easter bonnet from New Orleans. Chance said his daddy had turned his loss around and made another bundle of money. I was happy for them.

"Yes, ma'am," I said, "I like it." But the truth was, I still felt mixed up inside. I mean, there I stood on the gallery of the big house where Maman had grown up and that I'd been visiting all my life. But while we'd gained the big house, we'd lost 'Nonc Adolphe—'Nonc, who'd woken up this fever inside of me. I felt like I owed him my whole life.

The trade-off seemed too big to grasp. I had wanted things to change. But this was almost too much.

Paulo launched the kite I'd made for him to keep my long-ago promise. When I'd turned my knife over to Maman and confessed how I'd taken it, she'd folded it back into my hand. "We're making a new start, remember?" she'd said.

Now, in that same box on the mantel from which I'd kidnapped my knife lay the telegram we'd gotten from New Orleans. "Joined the Canadian Army," it said. "Gone to fight the war in Europe. Hope you'll be proud. Love, Adolphe."

Maman said novenas morning and night for 'Nonc Adolphe's safe return. I hoped the roads in Europe would lead him back home someday, and that he would find a good fiddle over there.

"Look, Stretch." Chance nudged my arm. "They're getting ready to play."

Sure enough, up on the gallery with its new coat of paint, Moïse Thibodeaux and Joseph Hébert had set up chairs and were pulling instruments out of cases.

"What you think?" said Chance.

I shot him a grin. "Last one there's a rotten Easter egg!" We raced to the porch. As Chance took out his accordion case, I went inside to get my fiddle.

I had a room all to myself now. And even though Paulo's room was right next door, the night was awful quiet without his snoring.

My hands shook as I opened my fiddle case, tuned the strings, and drew the bow across the cake of rosin. Moths fluttered in my stomach at the thought of standing up in front of all those people, no costume or mask to hide behind, to play my music.

But all I had to do was stare into the picture of my grandfather that Maman had given me to hang on the wall. He smiled at me through all the years that separated us. And there, tucked safely under his arm, was the very same fiddle that I now held in my hands. It still seemed like some kind of miracle, one that I couldn't quite wrap my mind around.

I stepped out onto the porch.

All eyes turned toward me, and people started clapping and whistling. "Come on, Félix!" they called, and *"Jouez, jouez!"* I looked at the other musicians and at Chance, who'd taken a seat at the far end of the group. Two guitar players stood, waiting for me to pick a song.

I set the fiddle onto my tender collarbone and lifted the bow above the strings. "I'd like to play a song I made up for my maman, Marie Olivier LeBlanc," I said. *"Bien merci pour tous.* Thank you for everything." Maman looked up at me from the yard and blew me a kiss.

As I pulled the bow across the strings, the music began to spin out of me like silk out of a spider. The song was a lively two-step. In between the notes lay all that had happened in the last few months—the anger and the joy, the heartbreak and the hope. And under that blew the breath of my uncle, of my grandfather, and of all those who'd come before us, all the way back to *Acadie*.

Maman and Papa danced a slow swirl together. Pretty soon other couples formed up in the yard, and friends and neighbors smiled and waved encouragement. Finally, I felt like everybody who looked at me could really see me for who I was, who I was still becoming day by day— son of André and Marie, nephew of Adolphe, brother of Paulo, but most of all me, Félix Octave "Stretch" LeBlanc.

When the song finally ended, Tante Mathilde winked up at me. "You think you're ready now, do you?"

I smiled. "I hope so."

"Firefly makes the light for its own soul," she said. I grinned at her. She was beginning to make sense to me.

"I knew you had it in you," said Monsieur Vidrine. "Just don't forget where you got your start."

"I won't forget," I said. "I made up this next one for you." When he flipped a quarter into my fiddle case, I shot him a grin, grateful that I could start paying Chance back what I owed him.

As I played the first notes of "Vidrine's Reel," old Jean Boutté let Paulo borrow his triangle, and he clanged along with the rest of us.

Tiny sprouts of cotton stuck their heads out of the Olivier fields, shimmering a bright new green in the spring sunlight. Paulo and I would help Papa tend the soil that my ancestors had worked so hard to own.

I wasn't giving up on seeing the big wide world. But for now, all I had to do was draw my bow over my fiddle strings to be transported far away, to places even an aeroplane couldn't take me.

Sometimes what you're looking for is right under your nose.

The afternoon spun by in song after song, dance after dance. At last the sun dipped behind the faraway trees, and the sky turned a brilliant violet and orange.

That night I put the sun to bed, as I would for many sunsets to come.

Glossary

assez: enough

bal: dance or ball

bien bon: good, great

bien merci pour tous: thank you very much for everything

boucherie: hog butchering

boudin: a sausage made with seasoned meat and rice

Caillette: common name for a spotted milk cow

capuchon: a tall pointed hat worn as part of rural Mardi Gras costumes

cochon de lait: suckling pig. Also a party where a roast pig is served as the main course

Comment ça va?: How are you?

courir de Mardi Gras: Mardi Gras run, when costumed riders travel the countryside asking for food

fiche-nous la paix: leave us alone

garçonnière: boys' bedroom, usually the large attic room in Cajun-style houses

garde-manger: food cupboard

gratons: cracklings, or pieces of fried hog skin

jambalaya: a thick mixture of rice, meat, and seasonings

jouez: play

Joyeux Noël: Merry Christmas

Glossary

"La Chanson de Mardi Gras": "The Mardi Gras Song"
(see page 166)
"La Valse du Bayou": "The Bayou Waltz"
lagniappe: a little something extra, a bonus
le bon Dieu: the Good Lord
le petit bonhomme janvier: the little January stranger, a
mythical figure who visits Cajun children on New
Year's Eve and leaves gifts in their shoes
les Américains: Americans (those who aren't Cajuns)
les maudits anglais: the blasted British
Madame: Mrs.
Madame Grands-Doigts: Mrs. Big Fingers, a mythical
figure who pulls the toes of naughty children in their
sleep
Mademoiselle: Miss
mais oui: but of course
Maman: Mama, Mother
Mardi Gras: Fat Tuesday, the holiday before the beginning of Lent
merci beaucoup: thank you very much
merci, bon Dieu: thank the Good Lord
mon ami: my friend
mon petit: my little one
Monsieur: Mr.
non: no
non, mon père: no, Father
'Nonc: Uncle (short form of **mon oncle:** my uncle)

oui, mon père: yes, Father

pâquer: to play a game of breaking Easter eggs against each other

parrains: godfathers

petit bébé: little baby

pop rouge: red soda pop

prie-Dieu: kneeler used for prayers

Qui c'est ça?: Who's that?

roux: flour browned in fat and used for thickening gumbos, gravies, etc.

Tante: Aunt

'ti boy: little boy ('**ti** is short for **petit**, which means "little." Cajun French often mixes English and French words.)

'ti fer: triangle (lit. "little iron")

traiteuse: faith healer (lit. "treater")

va-t'en: go on

Voulez-vous recevoir les Mardi Gras?: Will you receive the Mardi Gras riders?

"La Chanson de Mardi Gras"

Les Mardi Gras, ça vient de tout partout
Tout alentour, le tour du moyeu,
Ça passe une fois par an pour demander la charité
Quand même c'est une patate, une poule grasse ou
    des gratons.

Capitaine, Capitaine, voyage ton flag,
Allons chez l'autre voisin
Demander la charité pour vous-autres,
Vous-autres, vous venez nous rejoindre
Oui, au gumbo ce soir.

The Mardi Gras riders come from everywhere
From all around the neighborhood,
They pass by once a year to ask for charity
Even if it's just a sweet potato, a fat hen or some
    cracklings.

Captain, Captain, wave your flag,
Let's go on to the next neighbor's
To ask for charity for you all,
You all will come join us
Yes, at the gumbo tonight.